Whiskey Tango Foxtrot

Only the Dead Live Forever

By W. J. Lundy

Whiskey Tango Foxtrot

Only the Dead Live Forever

© 2013 W. J. Lundy

This book is a work of fiction. The names, characters, places and incidents are products of the writer's imagination or have been used fictitiously and are not to be construed as real. Any resemblance to persons, living or dead, actual events, locales or organizations is entirely coincidental. All Rights Are Reserved. No part of this book may be used or reproduced in any manner whatsoever without written permission from the author.

Edited by Monique Happy Editorial Services
http://www.moniquehappy.com

Dedicated to my family. My wife and daughter who do the hard work at home, and wait for me while I am away. If not for them I would have nothing worth working for, and nothing worth coming home to. And of course Mom and Dad you have always served as my biggest fans, encouraging me and providing the best advice, no matter how impossible it may seem. Thank you for setting the example.

1.

"Oasis, this is Talon, Oasis, this is Talon," the pilot, Captain Bradley, said over the radio, receiving only static as a response.

The Blackhawk flew low and fast over the dark churning waters of the Arabian Sea. There were flashes of light on the horizon from a developing storm. The helicopter's console flashed a warning that was audible in their headsets. They had been in the air for what seemed like hours. Brad had watched the co-pilot look at the warning light and reset it several times earlier, but now he was just ignoring it.

"You boys are going to want to keep those floatation devices handy. You may want to drop some of that body armor too, unless you're looking to sink to the bottom like a stone," Mr. Douglas, his co-pilot, said over the beeping of the alarm.

"Something you'd like to tell us, Sir?" Brooks asked with a sarcastic tone.

"We're having a bit of trouble contacting the platform and we're past bingo fuel; things may get wet here very soon," Captain Bradley answered over his headset.

Brad removed his tactical body armor and helmet and put on the inflatable flotation device. Sean and Brooks were making the same preparations. He watched the pilots scan the horizon; although they outwardly appeared very calm, he could see the worry on their faces. When Brad looked out of the window he understood why; he could barely make out the whitecaps of the sea below.

"Oasis, this is Talon ... Oasis, this is Talon," Bradley again called over the radio, still no response.

"There she is, at your eleven o'clock," Mr. Douglas motioned to the pilot.

Brad looked forward between the pilots seats. Far ahead he could begin to make out the shape of a huge object towering above the water. There was one red flashing beacon at the top of a long antenna; the rest of the platform was completely blacked out The platform columns projecting out of the sea appeared to have a number of vessels moored alongside them.

"Oasis, this is Talon... Oasis, this is Talon," Bradley called out again in frustration.

"We aren't getting any response from the platform. I'm going to make one pass around the rig and then we're going to have to land. We don't have much flight time left in the tanks," Bradley called out to all of them.

The helicopter slowed and passed a hundred yards off the starboard side of the platform, then circled around, flying counterclockwise and orbiting the rig. The platform was an impressive sight. It sat high above the water and boasted nearly three football fields of surface space on its large upper deck. Brad could see at least three levels of decks; the top one housed a number of cranes and towers. Three of the corners had distinct rust-colored steel building structures, while the open fourth corner was piled high with crates and industrial equipment. The helicopter landing pad was on piers elevated above the largest of the three building platforms.

The antenna tower light flashed a red beacon high above the rig, allowing them to see reflections off the window glass on the structure as they flew by them. There were no signs of movement on any of the decks; the rig appeared abandoned.

"It's go time. We don't have fuel to make it back to the coast, and there sure as hell won't be any water rescue coming for us, so I'm going to set us down," Bradley told them.

The helicopter pad was on the southwest corner of the platform. The pilot lined the Blackhawk up for an approach, began to slow it down, and then moved into a controlled hover. Brad looked out of the window and saw the dark landing pad emblazoned with a large letter 'H'. The landing pad was raised high above the other structures and was connected to the greater platform by a steel walkway. The floodlights on the walkway were all blacked out and the navigation lights that normally ringed the pad were off. The rig itself was silent and absent of movement.

"I'm bringing her in. Let's get frosty, guys; you may want to lock and load. I'm getting a bad vibe over this whole deal," Bradley said over the intercom.

All of the men had a bad feeling. Brad observed Sean and Brooks ready their weapons and pull down their night vision goggles as the helicopter slowly lowered to the landing pad. The helicopter landing gear made contact heavily with the deck. The pilots ran through checklists and began to power down the aircraft. Soon the turbines were idling down and there was nothing but the whipping sounds of the slowing blades. The pilots removed their headsets and harnesses, climbed over the center console, and moved into the rear part of the now silent helicopter.

"What are you thinking, Sir?" Sean asked in a low voice.

"I am really stumped, Chief, bordering on the verge of being very pissed off. I was told this place was manned by a platoon of Marines," Bradley answered. "Something is very wrong here."

"Hell yeah it's wrong! I wouldn't have taken this job if I'd known this would be what was waiting for us! I could still be in Bahrain, knee deep in cheap scotch," Mr. Douglas grumbled.

Sitting on the elevated landing pad and looking out the windows of the aircraft, they couldn't make out anything on the rig. In the distance they could see the occasional flash of lightning and hear the sound of thunder, making the current situation worse. The navigational windsocks were starting to blow and whip about at the tops of their poles, and the air had cooled considerably compared to what they had left in Afghanistan hours ago.

"Looks like we have a storm coming in," Sean whispered as his eyes studied the horizon.

"Chief, I'm going to need you and your men to secure the landing pad so Mr. Douglas and I can tie down the bird. We don't want to lose this aircraft if the winds pick up," Bradley said.

"Aye aye, Sir, just give the word," Sean said, obviously anxious to leave the helicopter and get to work.

Captain Bradley checked the slide of his M9 pistol to verify its readiness before securing it in its holster. He looked to Mr. Douglas who gave him a thumbs up.

"Okay, Chief we'll exit the same side. Mr. Douglas and I will secure the bird with the tie downs while you and your men pull security. Once everything is complete, we can meet up with you over there by the railing," Bradley said, pointing to a spot near the walk way entrance.

"Roger that, we are all over it," Sean said as he reached down and pulled the door open, letting in the cool damp night air.

Brooks exited first with his MP5 at the ready and turned right towards the tail of the aircraft. Brad came out next, followed by Sean. Brad moved past the nose of the aircraft and continued around it, securing the far side of the landing pad. Sean swept towards the nose and took a knee, scanning everything in his sector. When all of the men felt confident they were alone, one by one they said "clear" in low voices.

"Deck is clear, Sir," Sean said just above a whisper towards the Blackhawk's door.

The pilots stepped from the interior of the aircraft. Captain Bradley immediately placed chocks under the helicopter's wheels, while Mr. Douglas grabbed a stack of gear from the crew chief's position. Then the two men started applying tie downs to secure the helicopter to the deck. After they finished, Captain Bradley made a quick pass around the bird, verifying it was tied down to his satisfaction. When he felt everything was complete he moved to the rally point he had indicated earlier.

Sean moved to the pilot's location and took a knee. They were now overlooking the entire platform. They could see down the length of the walkway and to the landing below. The structures were all dark and there were no signs of life. The thunder was growing louder and the wind had begun to pick up. Sean looked to Bradley and whispered "What's the call, Sir?"

"There are fuel lines on the deck, but we will need power to use them. With that storm coming we won't be going anywhere for a while anyhow. I think we need to find shelter and find out what the hell is going on here."

"Let's move in a line down the ladder well. We'll secure the base, then scout from there," Sean said, then nodded at Captain Bradley as he continued. "I assume you know how to use that thing strapped to your hip, Sir?"

"It's been awhile but I think I'll figure it out," Bradley said drily, drawing his weapon. "Ready to move when you are, Chief."

"Brooks, take point; you fly boys, stay close behind me; Brad, you have rear security. We'll leave the heavy bags in the bird and come back for them later," Sean whispered. "Okay, unless there are any questions, let's get moving."

2.

Brooks slowly made his way down the long stairwell to the walkway below. Sean stayed in position at the top of the stairs, covering Brook's descent. The lightning had picked up its intensity and the winds were blowing harder. The team could hear the waves crashing against the structure's support pylons. Brooks cautiously reached the bottom, took a spot at the base of the stairs, and began searching in all directions. When he was confident it was clear, he signaled for Sean to proceed down.

Sean moved forward with the pilots behind him while Brad rotated into the over watch position. Sean stepped onto the landing and pivoted in the opposite direction of Brooks, then signaled for Brad to join them below. Brad took one last look at the compound from his elevated position; he saw nothing but the darkened structures and stirring sea waters in the distance. He stepped off quickly, made his way to the base of the stairs to rejoin the group, and took a knee beside Sean.

Then the sky opened up and the heavy rains came. Within seconds they were all soaked with the chilled water. The walkway at the base of the platform ran in two directions. Right led towards the open storage deck, and the left led down into the large structure under the helicopter pad. Sean signaled for Brooks to move the group toward the building.

Brooks wiped off his washed-out night vision goggles that were drowning in the torrential rain, and put on a large floppy boonie cap to shield them. Then he stepped off slowly with his MP5 at the ready. Brad stood wet and shivering at the back of the group, turning to look behind them as the team moved out. He had the feeling they were being watched, or that they at least were not alone. He tried to calm himself and turned to follow the rest of the group.

It was less than fifty feet to the first building. The entrance was barred by two large steel doors mounted on the face of a tall rigid steel wall. Sean moved forward to inspect the doors. Small round windows of wire-reinforced glass mounted in them met him at eye level, but for the time being Sean avoided exposing himself to them. He motioned for the pilots to wait near the wall while he called Brad and Brooks to stack up on the entrance.

Brooks formed up on the left side of the door with Brad behind him, while Sean stayed to the right. Sean reached forward and tried the door and found it unlocked. He then signaled to Brooks, who nodded in recognition, and then as quietly as he could, Sean eased the door open. When it was just wide enough for a person, Brooks swiftly moved into the room and cut to the right. Brad was right behind him and swept in to the left. Sean was the last one in and he stood in the doorway, scanning the entire length of the dark room.

They had entered into a large lounge; pool tables and sofas were overturned throughout the room. There was evidence of a battle; spent brass and blood trails were everywhere. The space was lit by low wattage emergency lighting so they could see the back of the room, where another set of large doors stood. Their safety-glass windows were shattered. Brooks moved towards them and checked the handle; finding them locked, he looked back to Sean and shrugged his shoulders.

"Okay guys, secure this space and get something to block that door. I'll bring in the officers," Sean whispered.

Brad and Brooks worked together to lift a large cabinet and sat it against the door at the back of the room to block themselves in. Sean walked through the entrance, trailed by the two soaking wet officers. He quickly secured the double doors and flipped the bolt locks, securing themselves in. Searching for lights but finding none, Brooks pulled on the emergency lighting lamps and pointed them down so a soft light filled the space.

Brad moved to a corner of the room and fell onto a large, overstuffed chair. Looking around the space, it appeared that a fight had broken out in the room; furniture was tossed around and the plasma TV screens were destroyed. A refrigerator in the corner had the door ripped open and it was knocked over and onto its face. "So where the hell are the Marines?" Brad asked no one in particular.

"They were supposed to be here," Bradley said. "This is really messed up. Do you still have your phone, Chief?"

"I already tried. I'm not getting a signal down here, probably too much steel in this building. I'll have to try again up by the helo after the weather clears. No point in us risking moving around in that shit right now," Sean answered.

He walked towards the now-barricaded doors. He tried looking through the spider-webbed glass, but found it impossible to see through.

"Brad? Brooks? You two up for some exploring?" he asked.

"Sure, why not? I was getting bored anyhow," Brooks said, getting to his feet and checking the magazine on his MP5.

Brad worked himself up out of the overstuffed chair and moved to the doors. Quietly, he helped Brooks pull the cabinets away from the entrance and stood behind the SEALs, waiting for direction.

"We're just going to check out this building and see if we can find out what's going on, Sir. You two block this door behind us and don't let anyone in," Sean said.

He pulled the small Jimmy bar and lock pick from his kit and started working the door. It was a heavy fire door designed to protect the space from intense heat, but the locks were not made to stop a determined thief. With a little bit of effort the seam in the door began to split, then the latch gave, popping just enough so that Sean could open the door a crack. There was nothing but darkness on the other side.

"You two ready?" Sean asked.

"Let's get to it," Brooks answered.

Sean slowly opened the door and Brooks slipped inside, followed by Sean, then Brad. Once they were through, the pilots quickly closed the doors and could be heard sliding furniture back against the opening.

Brad's night vision was powered up, and with his IR flashlight he could make out the greenish hue of a long hallway. Like the lounge they had just left, this hallway was scattered with random furniture and reams of office papers. There were mangled bodies in utility uniforms lying along the passageway, along with weapons and spent rounds to go with them. The space reeked of blood and cordite, and there were bullet holes and broken glass everywhere.

They took a few steps into the hallway, then knelt down to just listen and observe. All they could hear were the sounds of the storm outside. There was a subtle breeze coming from a broken window at the end of the long hallway, and an occasional lightning strike would briefly light the space, exposing the bodies to its ambient light. The floor was a glossy tile, now covered with blood that made the rubber soles of their boots feel sticky.

Brooks slowly got to his feet and stepped off, moving deliberately with his feet apart and his weapon at the ready. He lifted his feet high to step over the multitude of bodies and objects that littered the hallway. He moved past the first doorway, then posted up to allow Sean, who was directly behind him, to try the door. Finding it unlocked, Sean looked back and signaled for Brad to enter once the door was opened. Sean quickly opened the door and Brad moved though it to the left. Sean followed Brad, while Brooks held his position in the hallway, covering their backs.

Brad moved in and quickly checked all of the corners and dead spaces in the room; Sean did the same, working from the opposite direction. When they were confident the room was clear, they whispered to each other in low voices. This room looked untouched. There was a small desk in a corner with an office chair behind it, as well as a book shelf and filing cabinets against one wall. They rummaged through drawers and stacks of paperwork on the desk for information, but it seemed to be routine correspondence from the oil company PAK-PETRO to a middle manager, all of it dated before the outbreak.

As they moved back into the hallway, Sean placed his hand on Brooks' shoulder to indicate they were ready to move on. They cleared four more offices along the hallway in the same fashion, but still found nothing of interest. At the end of the hallway, they cautiously stacked up at a set of stairs. The window at the end of the hall was broken and, looking out, they could see the stormy waters of the sea. The rain was still coming down hard, and the broken window had allowed some of the rain to get in to soak the floor.

Brooks moved to the first step and noted that the stairs went up, then cut to the left at the first landing. When he reached the landing he turned partway, careful not to expose his entire body, then waited for Sean to move to his position, followed by Brad. Once they were all back online together, Brooks moved to the next landing. At the top of the stairs they found another door; this one was also hanging open.

Brooks again led the way into another long hallway that mirrored the one below them. Like before, once they were positioned in the hallway they all took a knee to listen for danger. Looking down this hallway, they found a tangled mess of bodies. Halfway down the length of the passage, positioned next to a door, lay a uniformed solder. His legs were missing, but the top half identified him as U.S. Marine Corps judging by the uniform jacket. The door itself had several bodies pressed up against its shattered window. Brooks pointed his IR laser at them to make sure the others had seen it.

Initially the sight made Brad want to turn around and go back down the stairs to the locked doors of the lounge. Before he had time to totally comprehend his circumstances, however, he saw Sean tap Brooks on the shoulder and signal for him to move out.

Again Brooks stepped past the first doorway and the piled bodies as Sean moved to the door and checked the handle. The lock was broken and had been pried from its frame. One by one, Sean grabbed at the bodies and pulled them aside. They hit the deck with a sickening thud. When the last body fell, a set of battered and broken blinds fell into place, keeping the men from being able to see into the room.

When Sean went to open the door, it swung inwards and he felt the resistance of furniture barricaded against it. He signaled for Brad to ready himself, then he pushed hard against it, using his leg against the wall for leverage. The door produced a gap just large enough for the two of them to slip into the blacked out room. Quickly they rushed in, and immediately heard the distinctive *click, click, click,* sound of a hammer falling on an empty chamber. Scanning the room, they saw the crumpled form of a female Marine in the far corner, pointing an empty pistol into the darkness and dry firing vainly.

Brad covered her while Sean verified the rest of the room was clear. Sean then turned his attention back to the Marine. She appeared uninjured, even though she was tucked back into the corner of the room with her knees drawn in. The room was very dark and it was obvious she couldn't see them. There was an M4 rifle next to her with a pile of empty magazines.

"Are you okay, Marine?" Sean asked in a low voice.

"Who ... who's there? Don't come near me," the startled Marine whimpered into the darkness, unable to see without the aid of night vision.

"It's okay Marine; we're not here to hurt you. We just came in a helicopter. We're here to help you," Sean lied.

"I think they're all dead. I don't know if there is anyone left ... except them," she said.

"Slow down, Marine, how long have you been here like this?" Sean asked.

"Last night ... This morning ... I don't know, the platform isn't safe, we have to leave," she whispered urgently.

"Can you walk?"

"Yes ... yeah ... I think so ... are we leaving?" she asked.

"Yeah, we're leaving, now let's get you on your feet," Sean said. "I know you can't see me, but I'm going to reach out and take your side arm for safe keeping. I promise I'll give it back, okay?"

She pulled the pistol in, then reconsidered and pushed it away with her outstretched arms. Sean took the M9 pistol and dropped it into a dump pouch attached to his belt. He then reached down, took the empty M4 from beside her, and passed it back to Brad. Brad pulled open the bolt, verified it was empty, and then slung it across his back.

"Okay Marine, I'm going to give you my hand and I want you to get to your feet and follow me out of the room, okay? I'm in here with another man and I have a third in the hallway. Don't be alarmed, we have you, okay?" Sean calmly spoke.

She nodded her head and Sean reached out his gloved hand. She took it and he pulled her to her feet. He asked her to grab onto the back of his jacket so he could lead her through the darkness. Sean and the Marine then slowly walked out of the room with Brad behind them. When he got outside, he signaled to Brooks that they were going back to the lounge. Sean took point this time and led them back though the hall and down the stairs. Brooks lagged behind, covering them as they moved.

When Brad made it back to the lounge door he quietly tapped it, then slapped at the door a bit louder when he didn't get a response. Eventually he heard a rustling from inside.

"Hey, is that you guys?" he heard Mr. Douglas call out.

"Yeah, can you open the damn door?" Brad said back.

He heard the officers drag the furniture out of the way and then they pulled the door open. Brad moved to the side and let Sean move through first, as he was still leading the way for the female. Then Brooks moved forward and into the lounge. Brad took one last look down the hallway before he slipped into the room to secure the door and help Brooks barricade it.

3.

They had the female Marine lay down on one of the long sofas that had been pushed against the wall. Once the sense of security finally hit her, she quickly collapsed and fell asleep. She was young, maybe mid-twenties, and she was small, barely over five feet, a hundred and ten pounds soaking wet. Once she had fallen asleep, Brooks gently inspected her for bites or scratches. Her uniform was filthy and torn, but she didn't appear to have any open wounds.

"She looks okay Chief, probably dehydrated though," Brooks said quietly.

"Okay good, thank you for taking care of that. So what do you think, you want to go back upstairs, continue the recon?" Sean asked.

"Hell no, Sean! Let's wait until she wakes up and gives us some info on what's going on here. It's a damn murder house up there," Brad said.

"I just don't feel good not knowing what we are sharing a building with. From the outside, it looks like there are no more than three, maybe four floors on this structure. I think it would be better if we could clear it. Especially since nothing or no one appears to know we're here," Sean said.

Captain Bradley stood and walked to the corner of the room to join the discussion. "That assumption makes no sense, Chief. The Blackhawk would have rattled this place coming in, and there's no way nothing heard it. If I had to guess, I'd say there's a mess of them hiding behind a door someplace, just waiting for you to open it."

"No, you can't go," the Marine said, struggling to sit up.

They all stopped and turned to look at her. "Oh, you're awake. How are you feeling?" Brooks asked.

"I'm a bit groggy and I feel like I got hit by a truck," she said. "Do you have any water?"

Brad walked across the room and reached into his pack, then handed her a bottle of water. She quickly twisted off the cap and guzzled down the entire bottle.

"Whoa, take it easy! We got to make that stuff last," Brad told her.

"Don't get stingy, Army, there are pallets full of water out on the storage deck," she spat back.

"Oh yeah? You want to go walk out there and grab some, Marine?"

"Oh … well, I guess you have a valid point there. So, ahh … any food?" she said as she put the cap back on the bottle.

Brad reached back into his pack and started opening his last can of the Afghan slop, which brought a smile to the faces of Sean and Brooks.

"What is that?" she asked.

Sean stepped forward and sat on a chair across from her. "Don't worry about it, you're going to love it, Corporal Swanson," he said.

"How did you know my name?" she demanded.

"It's written on your uniform, Corporal. You want to tell us what happened here?" Sean asked.

Brad finished opening the can, stuck his MRE spoon into the top of the mix, and handed it to her. "Sorry I can't heat that up for you, but trust me, it won't improve the taste anyhow."

Swanson took the can and scooped a large portion into her mouth before pausing. They thought she was going to turn green and spit it out, but after an uncomfortable silence she began to chew, then grudgingly took more. "This really is horrible, so thank you for sharing it with me," she said sarcastically.

Sean gave her an impatient look. "Back to where we left off. What is going on here, Corporal?"

"They must have gotten in on the PAK-PETRO boats. I don't know; it was in the middle of the night. I was sleeping in my cell when it started. Sergeant Johnson woke me up, told me to grab my kit because we were leaving."

"What do you mean, leaving?"

"He said the platform was breeched and we needed to fall back to the Edwards," Swanson said.

"Edwards?" Sean asked.

"The USS Edwards," she explained, "It's a submarine tender. It's been tied up here for a couple of weeks. We'd been replenishing it, getting ready to make a cruise back to the States."

"Okay, so then what?"

"I grabbed my gear and joined him in the hall. All of the housing cells are on the third deck; everyone was running around suiting up and heading below. There was a lot of screaming coming from the lower decks. Sergeant Johnson led the way, and when we made it to the first floor it was chaos. That's where they had gotten in. Our Marines were fighting hard, but most of them had already closed in on us and they were inside ..." She paused; a haunted look came across her face. "It was hand-to-hand."

"What did you do?" Sean probed.

"They were already through the lounge and into the hallway. One of the Marines in the middle of it managed to lock the lounge door, but too many of them had already gotten in. Sergeant Johnson and I tried to make it back to the third level but someone had secured the doors at the bottom of the stairs and they wouldn't open them."

"So you got caught in the middle?"

Nodding, she continued. "We ran back to the second floor stairway ... they were pouring in up the stairs ... we fell back into the hallway. Johnson was firing at them, knocking them down, but there were just too many," she said as her voice started to crack. "He shoved me into the office and told me to barricade the door."

"And?"

"I locked the door ... I pushed the desk against it and hid. I heard them coming for him. He fought them, and I heard him scream ... it took a long time ... but they didn't leave, they started pounding on the office door, they broke the glass and tried to get in. I fired my rifle till it was empty, then I reloaded and fired more. When my rifle was done, I fired the pistol. I ran out of ammo and waited for them to come in after me ... but ... but something happened ... They were distracted. I heard them crash through the doors and go up to the third deck. They never came back."

"Do you know where they came from?"

"No! I told you already! I was asleep. Some of the men were yelling and blaming it on PAK-PETRO, since they own and operate these oil rigs. They had been pulling people back from the other sites all month, consolidating them here ... waiting for the main evacuation order.

"Everyone is supposed to get checked for bites and scratches, but sometimes people get through the cracks. We've found primals turned in their cells before, screaming and trying to get out ... Plus there are a lot of people in the ships moored below and on the first level; they don't get checked till they get to the second deck."

"Another classic cluster fuck," Brooks said in frustration. "Who was in charge of security here?"

"Officially the Marines were, but there were only twenty-five of us. There were over five hundred people on the platform plus I don't know how many on the ships. And we aren't grunts; most of us are wrench turners and technicians. We had to trust the locals to do most of the security since we were only in charge of the top deck. PAK-PETRO ran the lower two decks with the Pakistani Navy; they have a few boats down there. *Our* Navy never left their ships, they just plugged into the platform for shore power."

"So to sum it up, we have no idea what's going on anywhere on this platform, how many infected there are, or how many survivors," Sean grunted.

4.

They sat in silence and tried to digest the bad news. Swanson was asleep again. They still had plenty of questions for her, but Sean didn't see any point in beating her up all night. They were locked into the lounge, but still felt uneasy when they stared at the door that led into the building, not knowing what waited for them on that third deck.

Brad had collected his gear and was back in the overstuffed chair in a corner. He had broken down his rifle and was meticulously cleaning it. Brooks distracted himself by doing the same in the opposite corner of the room. Sean lay down to sleep on a pool table; the pilots were already sleeping against the front wall on a pile of sofa cushions that they had bunched together. The emergency lighting was still working, but they had no idea how long the batteries would last.

Dawn came slowly; the rain was still coming down hard. The grey gloomy light was just beginning to pierce the glass windows in the door when Sean got to his feet and peeked out of the glass. Looking both ways as best he could, he seemed satisfied that the immediate outside was clear.

"Brooks, Brad, why don't you two start suiting up," Sean said.

"What are you thinking, Boss?" Brooks asked.

"I want to take a quick look around so we can get our bearings. We also need to pull the gear and ammo from the Blackhawk," Sean answered. "Captain, you two stay here with Swanson and hold the fort. We won't be long. Keep an eye on those doors."

"Okay, can do, Chief," Bradley answered.

The team suited up and gathered at the double doors. Sean pulled the bolt back and slowly opened the right side, slicing his viewpoints until he had a full view of everything to his left. Then Brooks eased open the opposing door and sliced to the right. When they were confident the way was clear, the left door was closed and they slid outside before closing the right door behind them. They heard the officers latching the door locked.

They stood tight against the wall, looking in all directions. The rain was still coming down hard but the thunder had faded. They could hear the waves crashing against the ships and the pylons below. Normally, the ships would have untied and taken the storm in open waters instead of being thrashed against the platform, but there must not have been anyone to pilot them.

Sean looked down at the deck and grimaced. "I hope those vessels aren't doing permanent damage to the structure. We're in bad enough shape as it is."

Brooks lifted his rifle and scouted the area beyond the building with his optics. "I don't see any movement, Chief, and the far walkway looks clear."

"We don't have the manpower to leave a guard here to cover our six, so we'll just need to keep our heads on swivel," Sean warned.

They turned and slowly patrolled toward the helicopter pad, stopping often to listen and check their back trail. It was hard to hear anything through the pouring rain and the sounds of the water beating off the steel buildings. The floor was made up of rigid steel grates; even so, it was hard to see through the tangle of pipes to the working spaces below.

The path back to the flight deck was clear; they could just barely see through the rain to the landing. Blowing rain was washing across the metal deck grating. The winds rolled the wash up and blew it across the deck at them. They were already soaked in the chilled water. Brad had removed his goggles and was wearing a fleece watch cap. He held his rifle at the ready and tried to stay in position just behind Brooks as they slowly made their way down the walkway.

They reached the landing and, after a brief pause, Brooks made the turn around the corner, with Sean and Brad behind him. They found the helicopter just as they had left it. They moved about the landing pad and used the elevated position to survey the platform. Even in the stormy conditions they were able to see a great deal more than they had the night before.

They could clearly see down onto the storage deck where a large number of crates and plastic containers were neatly stacked in rows. There were obvious signs of a battle on the deck. The dead were scattered about and concentrated near a hasty barricade, close to what appeared to be another staircase leading to the second deck. There were two other metal buildings on the two remaining corners of the platform; one appeared be a control building containing large windows, and the other was only a two-story with no windows.

The southwest apron of the helicopter pad leaned out over the edges of the platform. By pushing up against the railing, they were able to see hundreds of feet below to the crashing sea. There was no large submarine tender as the Marine had suggested. They could see a couple of Pakistani-flagged fast attack boats, a few tugs labeled with the PAK-PETRO logo, and a larger civilian fishing boat. All of the vessels appeared to be dead in the water and were taking a beating in the storm.

Sean tried the satellite phone; even though he was pulling a strong signal, he couldn't get an answer. Frustrated, he powered it down and stowed it back in his assault pack.

They opened the doors to the helicopter, quickly loaded the large rucks onto their backs, and stacked up to make the return trip to the lounge. Brooks was partway down the stairs to the first landing when his fist shot in the air. Brad struggled to kneel on the uneven surface of the stairs, battling the weight of his pack as he strained to turn his head to see what had alerted Brooks. Far in the distance he spotted it.

"Oh fuck," he gasped.

There was a small pack of ten to fifteen primals gathered below them near the entrance to the lounge. So far they hadn't been alerted, or they would have been moaning. The team froze on the stairs and watched the pack. The primals had gathered outside of the lounge. One of them seemed to be the leader. It was larger than the rest and wore part of a Marine Corps utility uniform. Its face had been torn open above the cheekbone, and a large portion of its scalp was missing, but it didn't seem at all bothered by the wounds. It slapped at the steel doors of the building but quickly lost interest and started to make its way closer to the team's current position. Quickly and quietly they backtracked up the stairs and to the landing pad.

"Stay quiet. If we start a fight, we have no place to fall back to," Sean whispered.

When they returned to the pad, they silently dropped their packs and laid flat on the deck, trying to hide. They could see through the drainage slots in the decking to the walkway below. The primals were still moving slowly along the path, presumably following the leader that had been pounding on the lounge door. The rains were still soaking everything, but the primals seemed unaffected by the downpour. When they made it to the landing they stopped and appeared to contemplate climbing the stairs. The primals stirred back and forth as they decided on a path. The leader lashed out at another member of the pack with a screech, and they moved on towards the storage deck.

When it was again clear, the three men stacked back up and moved down the stairs. At the landing, they quickly checked for signs of the pack and thankfully found none. The primals seemed to have moved on beyond the storage deck. The team quickly rounded the landing, headed down the final steps, and back to the lounge. They moved past the double doors and waited. Sean tapped a pre-arranged code at the steel door and waited for a response from inside. Brad had moved past the entrance and was covering forward, while Brooks was still looking through his rifle back toward the stairs to the landing pad.

Brad stepped away from the wall and turned to look back at Sean. Sean was visibly frustrated, tapping at the door in the code and waiting for the officers to unlock it. He paused, and hearing no response, tapped again. Brad shook his head, then turned back to the front ... and gasped in shock.

He found himself face to face with one of the largest primals he had ever seen. Before Brad could raise his rifle to fire, the primal lunged at him. The impact of the thing and the weight of his pack threw Brad hard to the ground.

They landed awkwardly on the deck. Brad fell crunched against his large rucksack in a half sitting position, with the primal grabbing at his clothes. Brad grabbed its neck; pushing it away with his right gloved hand, he buried his thumb into the soft tissue of its chin while his fingers gripped its throat. His free left hand was battling with the primal for wrist control as he wrapped his legs around the creature and tried to pull it tightly into his guard; locking his legs, he then held on for dear life.

At the sound of the commotion, Sean turned. Afraid to fire a shot and risk hitting Brad, he leapt past them and threw himself onto the back of the creature, placing it into a strong rear choke hold. Sean had the choke in deep and was pushing the thing's head forward for all he was worth. With the down and forward pressure relieved from him, Brad was able to dig a heel in to the creature as he maintained control of the primal's left arm. He rolled hard and pulled himself into a sloppy arm bar. Not waiting for a tap, he applied maximum pressure and felt the elbow joint break and dislocate.

Without the strength of both arms, the primal fell flat on its face with Sean still securely on its back, its last good arm wildly flailing. Brooks grabbed Brad by the straps at the top of his pack and pulled him away from the beast. With the tight choke applied, the primal was unable to scream or moan. Sean applied more and more pressure but the creature failed to die. Finally, Sean crushed its wind pipe and rolled hard; the creature's neck made an audible crack as its spine was broken. Sean held tight as the primal's body stiffened violently, then went slack.

Sean slowly released his grip from the primal and rolled away from it. He looked down and saw that its eyes were still following him with a hateful glare. Even with its windpipe crushed and its neck and spine snapped, the primal still was looking to fight. Brooks pulled a small suppressed MKII pistol from his pack and placed it against the creature's head, then fired a single shot.

Suddenly the door opened and Captain Bradley looked out. "What the hell are you guys doing out here making all of that noise?" He stopped and looked down at the dead primal, and both Brad and Sean still sitting on the deck. "Oh! Well hey, come on guys, get back inside before more of them come."

5.

The men hurried into the room, the Captain quickly locking the doors behind them. Shivering from the cold and soaked to the bone, they began stripping off their uniforms.

"Err, ah, excuse me! There is a lady present," Swanson snarled.

"Oh, please feel free to wait outside while we avoid hypothermia," Sean barked back.

Swanson had no reply and instead pulled a heavy chair and turned it so that it faced the wall, then sat down. Mr. Douglas stepped forward and retrieved the wet uniforms from the floor and started hanging them to dry, while Captain Bradley handed the men some folded linens that he had found in a cabinet. The room was still dimly lit by the emergency lighting and the winds were howling outside.

"When will this damn rain end?" Brad said, mostly to himself while wrapping a sheet around his naked body.

"What? This rain won't be over for a while, few days maybe ... That's a tropical cyclone out there, and just the beginning of it. They were predicting a Category 3 at least. That's why the squids were prepping the tender to get us the hell out of here," Swanson answered, still facing the wall.

Captain Bradley rolled his eyes and looked her way "Bullshit! Cyclone? Colonel Cloud didn't say anything about a cyclone when he briefed me on our exfiltration plan."

"Of course he didn't ... once we delivered Aziz, we weren't his concern anymore. So when was the tender supposed to leave? Where did it go?" Brooks said.

"I'm not sure. I know the sailors were anxious to get out ahead of the storm. I already told you PAK-PETRO's been moving survivors from the other rigs to here over the last couple days. We were just waiting on the word to get going ... but then the attack ... I don't know what happened. Maybe they're still down there waiting for us; we need to get down to the dock level!"

"Don't worry about it. The tender is gone. All I saw in the water were Pakistani boats," Sean said as he fell onto the end of a sofa.

"So what now then?" asked Mr. Douglas.

"Now I say we need to clear this damn building. I'm not spending another night in here not knowing what's up on that third deck," Sean said.

"How do you plan to do that?" asked Mr. Douglas.

"Well, I figured I'd take a quick break; then we'll go out that there hallway and up those stairs and kill everything that doesn't look friendly," Sean said, pointing at the doors leading from the lounge and into the building.

"What the hell? Are you serious?" Swanson argued.

"I'm not willing to just sit here until we starve ... From my last count, Brooks, Brad, and I are the only ones with any gear or food. We're cut off from the supplies on the deck, and our current position is occupied. Unless anyone has any better ideas, everybody be prepared to assault through this building in two hours, and I mean *everybody!*" Sean gritted, looking in the direction of the two officers.

"Excuse me Chief, but we aren't trained for this," Mr. Douglas said, stepping forward.

"Doesn't matter anymore; we're all in this together now. We're all going to pull our weight until we get out of here. Swanson, tell me more about the platform, how many were on board?" Sean asked.

Captain Bradley got to his feet and took a step towards Sean, holding his hand up towards Swanson. "Hold up Chief, I know you are not happy, but rushing to decisions and pushing us forward isn't going to solve anything right now."

Completely ignoring the Captain's words, Sean said, "Sir, with all due respect, the next time I knock on a door you better move your ass and answer it! You almost got Brad and I killed out there while you took your sweet ass time unlocking that door. Consider this fair warning. I suggest you ready your weapons; *we* will be taking this building back in two hours. Now Swanson, what do we know about the platform?"

Captain Bradley moved back to his seat and sat heavily without saying a word. Swanson looked around the room, but realizing there would be no support if she continued the argument, she began to explain what she knew to Sean.

"Well, this is the housing and business block; it used to house the trades guys, pipe fitters, welders, rough necks, stuff like that. We moved all of the military in here. There were only about fifty of us in total. There are three floors; first two are offices, and the top floor is housing cells. Twelve rooms and an open lounge. The helipad is on the roof."

"Food? Water?"

"Yeah, there's a stocked galley upstairs, but the water is off until we get the lights back on."

"And next door?" Sean questioned.

"The next building over is the controls unit. It houses the radio tower and most of the switches for the platform's equipment. The far corner facility is the power station; it has generators and such. That's where I worked. We kept the power plant running and it must be abandoned now. I'm sure that's why the lights are out," Swanson finished.

"Can you get the power back on?"

"Yeah sure, easy, I'm sure the tanks just ran dry. I'll just need some help switching over the barrels ... this place has plenty of fuel on hand," Swanson said.

"What's below us?" Sean asked.

"That's the industrial deck. We didn't go down there much, since PAK-PETROL was in charge of that space. They've been housing all of their people there. The very bottom deck was where they were loading and offloading crews from the ships."

"Okay, clear as mud then. Alright everyone, get your gear together. Be ready to move out in two hours," Sean said as he started to break down his MP5 for another round of cleaning.

Brad leaned back in his chair. He was extremely frustrated and sore from his battle on the deck with the primal. He had no interest in Sean's plan to clear the building, yet he understood completely the importance of the mission. If they were going to survive, they would have to regain their ground. He wouldn't argue the decision. Brad knew it was the right thing to do, even if it wasn't the easiest.

He dug through his bag, pulled out a fresh set of MultiCams and got dressed. He grabbed his rifle and inspected it. He hadn't fired it in a few days, but still he removed the bolt and oiled all of its components. He checked and double-checked his magazines. He still had close to a combat load's worth of ammo, and there were still hundreds of rounds in his rucksack. Grabbing his vest, he made sure everything was secure and then placed his last fresh set of batteries into his night vision goggles.

Once Brad was confident he would be ready for the coming mission, he leaned his head back deep into the chair and pulled his patrol cap over his eyes.

6.

When he opened his eyes, Brad saw Sean trying to look through the glass of the doors leading into the hallway. Brooks was standing behind him, readying his weapons and attaching gear to his chest harness. Swanson was leaning over her boots, tucking in the laces; her M4 was sitting beside her. Both officers were also up digging through their small flight bags.

Even though Brad was far from his normal routine, he still followed a mental checklist when he prepped for a mission. He went through his checklist, physically touching each item. He tightened all of his loose straps and checked to make sure his spare magazines were loaded and snapped in place. His fighting knife was hanging just below his left shoulder, with the handle down. A tourniquet was on his right shoulder, a first aid pouch on his belt. He wore his M9 on his hip, and the holster held two spare magazines.

Brad finished his prep work, drank down an entire bottle of water (never knowing when the next chance to hydrate would come), then relieved himself into the empty bottle and tossed it into a trash can. He was ready to go, so he made his way to Sean and Brooks and leaned against the wall. Sean pulled four small cardboard boxes of 5.56 NATO rounds from his backpack and tossed them to Swanson.

"Load these up, Corporal; you may need them," Sean said.

He then turned and faced the group. "We're going to move out in two groups. Brooks, Brad, and I will push forward on the assault team. I want you three to wait until we make the first landing, then move in behind us as support. I want separation in the teams. Only one team at a time on a floor or in a ladder well. We will assault forward; you three will lag back and be prepared to reinforce us if we need to fall back in a hurry or get blocked. Corporal, you are in charge of the support team. Any questions?"

"So we're supposed to just stand around in the hallway and wait for you to do something?" Mr. Douglas asked.

"Sir, I would recommend you get into defensive positions at every stop. Odds are, if we fall back, we'll be moving in a hurry. Just please try very hard not to shoot us," Sean answered.

Captain Bradley moved towards the door and unholstered his M9. "Okay Chief, let's get this over with."

Sean looked at Brooks and signaled for him to move out. Brooks slowly opened the door, clearing everything in his vision as it slowly revealed the interior of the hallway. Brad moved forward and took a position inside the hallway and on the left wall. Brooks moved a step ahead and took the right wall, with Sean holding the center of the hallway.

With the door now fully open and the light of the lounge bleeding into the hall, they knelt down and listened for any movement. The hallway was as they had left it, covered with trash and bodies and stinking of death. The assault team moved forward and stacked up on the first office door. Swanson's support team stepped to the lounge's doorframe and took a knee to watch Sean's team work.

Even though the first floor offices had been cleared the day before, they were cautious and had decided beforehand that they would do a one hundred percent sweep of everything. The assault group would clear the room and push forward, while the support team would occupy their previous position to make sure nothing got past them. Slowly they cleared the first floor and stacked on the ladder well at the end of the hall.

Brooks cracked a chemical light and dropped it at the base of the stairs. None of the support team wore night vision, and he didn't want them to get spooked and pop off a round in the dark. Brooks waited for Sean and Brad to stack behind him. A single tap on his shoulder indicated they were ready, so he crept up the dark stairs. His night vision goggles painted the space a creepy digital green. He paused often to listen for movement, but all he could hear was the creaking of the metal structure and the storm blowing outside.

He reached the top and looked down the long, dark corridor. It looked the same as they had left it; the dismembered Marine still lay in the center of the hallway. The stack of primal bodies was still piled in front of the open office door. He slowly led them forward, trying to be quiet, although their boots slipped and squeaked on the sticky, blood-covered floor; occasionally they kicked spent brass and heard the clinking of metal on metal.

Again they cleared the rooms. The trio made it past the point where they had found Swanson. They moved to the end of the hall and stacked on the door leading up to the unknown third floor. They held up and waited, hearing the rustling of the support team moving up the stairs and taking positions at the far end of the hallway. Brad turned to look at them, barely making out their facial expressions in the hue of the night vision goggles.

He could see the silhouettes of Swanson and Mr. Douglas as the two of them peeked out and down the hallway toward him. The captain must have held back to cover their six. He watched Swanson take a step out of the ladder well and take a knee with her M4 held at the ready, while Mr. Douglas stood at a crouch just over her shoulder.

Brad felt the pat coming from Sean to his front and knew it was time to move again. He tapped Sean back to indicate he was ready, and they moved forward to the doors leading to the third floor. Brad watched Brooks reach for the handle of the door. Unlike the others, this one was in a locked position but it had been bashed in, twisted at its hinges, allowing one of the sections to be forced inward off of its frame. There was an imploded gap where the creatures had breached the doorway, and the metal edges were covered with ripped pieces of clothing and skin.

Brooks wrapped his gloved fingers over the edge of the door and applied pressure to open it. The door started to screech as the twisted steel pieces pulled against each other. He immediately stopped and stepped back. He moved back to Sean and whispered, "The door is completely jammed up. I can open it, but it's going to be loud."

"Okay. We'll rip it open, but use the rope and give us some standoff distance," Sean whispered back.

Brooks reached into his butt pack and pulled out a length of heavy corded rope. He lashed it around the handle of the door, then they backtracked down the hall, letting the length of the rope out behind them as they went. They stopped just in front of the support team. Sean and Brad took a knee on opposite sides of the hall and aimed the IR lasers of their weapons at the battered doors. Sean nodded to Brooks to pull the rope.

Brooks yanked the rope and the door let out a wailing screech of twisted sheet metal, but the door didn't give. He pulled again, making a lot of noise but no better results. Without instruction, Bradley moved forward from the ladder well and grabbed a section of the rope from Brooks. Together they strained and pulled, the door screeching all the more. Brad watched as the door began to give under the weight of the rope, but the handle section buckled and the rope sprang free.

Brooks shook his head and pulled the rope back towards him, coiling it as he reeled it in. "Hold position and cover me, I'll tie it back on," Brooks whispered. Sean nodded his acknowledgement and Brooks started to slowly make his way back to the door. Only two steps into the walk they heard a crash coming from the third deck's ladder well. Brooks froze in place, dropping the rope and readying his weapon. Then they heard the first of many moans …

"Ahhh shit, there goes the neighborhood," Brooks said as he stepped back and returned to the assault team's formation.

"Captain, get back to your team," Sean said.

Just as Bradley turned to move, the first primal crashed into the set of battered doors. Brad raised his rifle and watched the doors heave. Sean fired carefully placed rounds that pierced the metal doors, but the commotion on the far side continued.

"Concentrate your fire on the doors! Let's kill these fucks while they're trapped on the landing," Sean said.

Brooks and Brad acknowledged the order by firing shots in groups of two into the doors at shoulder height. They saw more rounds pierce the door, but the pounding continued and the intensity of the moaning grew. Soon the hall was filled with smoke and the visibility had dropped. They continued to fire straight down the hallway into the moans, filling the doors and landing with a wall of lead.

Brad felt the bolt in his rifle lock to the rear and called out, "Reloading!"

He quickly dropped his magazine and fished a fresh one from his vest. Brad pushed the bolt release and slammed the forward assist with the palm of his hand. Before he could tell the others he was back online, they heard the crunch of the doors giving way and the frenzied charge of the primals.

They broke from the smoke and quickly closed the distance, rushing at them in a thick pack, filling the hallway and moving fast. The assault team fired at them, knocking down the first rank and slowing the charge as the falling primal bodies impeded the mass. Without being asked, Swanson moved her support team forward. They took up a standing position behind Brad. He could hear the officers' 9mm pistols join the fight and he could feel the brass from Swanson's rifle bounce off his shoulder as she fired into the mob.

One of the creatures broke through and dove at the men, landing on top of Brooks. Brooks pushed up his forearm and pressed the creature's face against the wall as he was forced over and onto his side. Captain Bradley stepped forward and gripped the primal by the back of its collar to pull it away from Brooks. With Brook's forearm still pressing it tightly against the wall, Bradley shoved his pistol against the primal's temple and fired.

Brooks rolled from under the creature and forced himself back into a firing position, returning his weapon to action. Brad focused his attention forward as another wave moved at them en masse. He fired nearly point-blank into the mob, smoke and the flash of the weapons washing out his night vision.

Sean yelled "Weapon dry!" and seamlessly pulled his sidearm, pumping heavy .45 caliber rounds into the charging primals. The front rank's heads exploded as more pushed them forward and into the team. Then the fight fell apart. Swanson screamed that she was out of ammo and she started backpedaling into the stairway. A primal leaped from the mob's ranks, hitting Brad square. Another jumped against the wall, skirted the fire and bounced into Sean's blind spot.

Both men were knocked off of their feet and began fighting for their lives in the confined space. Swanson and Douglas had both pulled back. Bradley leapt forward to help Sean while Brooks focused his fire forward, trusting his brothers to regain their position and knowing if he stopped firing to help them they would be completely overrun.

Brad was crushed against the floor and could feel the primal gnawing at the sides of his helmet. Brad released the grip on his rifle and strained for his pistol with his right hand but it was jammed under his thigh. He forced his left arm between the creature and his chest and pulled his fighting knife, then forced it into the primal's arm pit.

He shoved the blade all the way to the hilt, feeling it grind against the bone. The creature continued to fight, so Brad reversed his grip on the blade and pushed the knife deeper, twisting the handle as he shoved through muscle and bone. He felt the primal's grip weaken. Brad took advantage of the opportunity and forced his right arm up, rolling the primal off of him and to the side. He drew back the knife and shoved it forward at a deep angle into the primal's neck, piercing its brain stem and skull.

With the primal down, Brad looked forward and saw two more closing on him fast. He regained control of his rifle and fired quick shots to knock them down. He turned just in time to see Sean finish the creature he was wrestling with two rapid shots to the skull, the heavy rounds blowing chunks of bone and blood into the wall beside him. Bradley dropped back against the wall into a sitting position, breathing hard.

Then it was quiet; nothing but the sounds of post-firefight breathing and sizzling brass on the bloody floors. Brooks reloaded his weapon before reaching down and pulling Brad back into a kneeling position. Sean climbed to his feet and looked down the hallway, using the beam of his laser to probe the fallen pile of primals. The sound of boots behind them indicated that the support team was moving back to the hallway.

Brad was breathing hard; his hands and knees were shaking from the rush of adrenalin. He was still feeling the high of the fight when he heard the sounds of boot treads on the stairs. He turned just in time to see the support team getting back into position behind them. Sean looked back and asked Captain Bradley if he was okay. The captain gave a nod and climbed back to his feet.

Sean stared at Swanson and Mr. Douglas. "Captain Bradley, I appreciate you coming forward in the middle of that for me; I saw you help Brooks as well. Thank you."

"I'm just trying to show you my old ass isn't completely useless when it's not strapped to a helicopter."

"Everyone check yourselves and get me a thumbs up," Sean said.

Brad looked himself over, finding his armor was covered with blood and gore. He had burnt through half his ammo in the small engagement and he knew they wouldn't be able to keep up this tempo without resupply. He pushed himself to his feet and stretched, noting he wasn't injured, just sore. He looked over at Sean and gave him a thumbs up.

The hallway ahead now had a mound of bodies covering it; the dead were everywhere and the stench of blood and cordite was still heavy in the air. It was dark again, and the only sound was that of the storm outside breaking the silence. Sean started to push forward with Brooks on the opposite side of the hallway; they were both stepping carefully over the dead primal bodies. Brad fell in behind them, carefully watching where he placed his feet, still wary of the creatures covering the floor.

The double doors leading to the third floor stairway were now completely opened. Broken, bent, and twisted from their frame, but open. Brooks approached the landing and peeked inside. He signaled back that the first approach was clear, and Sean signaled for him to proceed. Sean fell in behind him with Brad taking the rear position.

The stench in the stairway was overwhelming. Brad pulled his shemagh up over his face but it did little to filter the smell of death and human waste. Brooks made his way to the top of the stairs and cut the angle, carefully making the turn to the next set of stairs. The team stayed tight, following him to the top. At the landing to the third floor they found another set of doors. It was no surprise that they had also been pushed in off their frame.

The room beyond the doors was lit in low light from the emergency floodlight box hanging on the wall. Sean gave a signal and they moved into the room, dividing it into sectors, and verifying it was clear. They found themselves in a lounge identical to the one downstairs, except this room had been torn apart. The walls were covered in gore; pool tables and furniture were overturned and piled as if they had been used in a hasty barricade. There was just the one emergency light left, located high up on the wall; the rest had been torn from their boxes

"What in the hell happened here?" Brad whispered.

"Looks like they made a last stand before they were overtaken," Sean said.

Brooks made his way to the back wall where the double doors exiting the lounge at the far end of the room were still secured. "Maybe not," he said. "These doors are still locked."

Sean and Brad stepped forward and examined the solidly locked doors. They discovered that these doors were the same as the ones on the first floor: two heavy steel fire doors designed to contain three thousand degree fires for hours, not just to divide spaces like the other flimsy sheet-metal doors. The wire-reinforced safety glass was shattered and impossible to see through.

The support team crept up the stairs and made their way into the low glow of the emergency lighting. Swanson moved forward into the room. "They locked us out. This is where we tried to fall back to before …. The bastards locked us out and left us to die."

Sean looked away from her and back to the sealed fire doors. He pounded a fist against them and heard nothing. He picked up a piece of broken metal from a table leg and began tapping against the steel frame of the door. He tapped a rhythmic beat that in no way would be confused with the pawing of a primal. Sean paused, then shook his head. "Fuck it." He pounded on the doors. "Hey assholes, open the damn doors!" he yelled.

7.

There was a rustling of noise on the other side. Sean pounded and yelled again, "I can hear you in there, now open this door!"

"Get away from here or we'll open fire," came a frightened voice on the other side of the door.

"The hell you will! Now open this door before I place a charge on it and blow it off of its hinges!"

"We aren't letting anyone in. You're all infected."

"No, we came in on the helicopter; you had to have heard it. We landed on the helipad above the building. Now open this door! That's an order!" Sean roared.

"No, it's impossible, everyone's dead, there's nothing left outside, and you're ... you're all infected!"

Swanson stepped forward and stood next to the door. "Wilson? Is that you? This is Corporal Swanson ... it's true ... these guys came in on a helicopter. They killed them all and they rescued me."

"Swanson? How ... you were with the group that was attacked downstairs. *How are you even alive?"*

"I'll explain later. Can you just open the door? You can inspect us if you want, check us for bites. We're all clear, Wilson, please just let us in."

There was a long pause followed by muffled voices and arguing going on inside. After a few long painful moments they finally heard furniture moving and bolts clicking and snapping on the other side. The handle turned and the door opened in.

When the door opened they saw the face of a young, red-haired Marine. There was another Marine right beside him pointing a rifle at Sean. "Okay, we opened the door, but you ain't coming in without an inspection," the red-haired Marine said.

"Okay son, you can look us over, but if your buddy doesn't lower his weapon you'll be helping him extract pieces of it from his ass for the next week," Sean said in a calm voice.

The Marine looked back to his buddy with the rifle. "It's okay Ben, you can lower your weapon." Turning back to Sean he said, "Okay, you first then, put your arms up and turn around."

Sean followed his instructions and, after a quick rundown, they had all passed the Marine's cursory inspection. He told them they could come into the room and waited for all of them to pass through the doorway before he closed the double doors and bolted them shut.

They found themselves standing in a hallway twice the width of the ones below. The walls had evenly spaced doors going down both sides and two latrines located at the end of the hallway. Brad made his way into the dark hallway and leaned against the wall as he watched Sean walk in behind him. Sean moved past Brad and stopped, turning to face the red-haired Marine again.

"Alright Marine, who's in charge up here?" Sean asked

"Well, nobody I guess. I'm Private Harry Wilson. This is Private Ben Walkens," the red-haired Marine said, pointing to the man beside him. "Those two over there are Private Craig and Private Nelson, the civilians are Bill and Tony."

The men in the room all nodded as they were introduced. Two of the men were older and dressed in civilian clothes (obviously Bill and Tony). Sean made similar introductions of his team.

"So how is it you managed to get yourself barricaded behind these doors?" Sean asked.

Swanson stepped forward and got in Wilson's face. "Yeah, explain to me *why the fuck* you didn't open the doors! You killed us; *you got Sergeant Johnson killed*!" she screamed.

"Hey! That's not our fault!" Wilson yelled. "The lieutenant ordered us to barricade those doors when the rest of you assaulted down the stairs. He said we had to hold this position. He told us to lock the doors and we weren't to open them for anybody except him. He said you might all be infected and we couldn't trust anyone."

Private Walkens added, "It's true, Corporal, we thought you had all left us to die. We didn't want to lock y'all out; honest, we were just following orders."

Sean looked at him, shaking his head. "Just following orders? Okay, whatever, so what have you been doing to improve your situation over the last three days?"

Wilson looked around, but nobody seemed eager to speak. "Well, uhh, we've kinda just been hanging back. We figured someone would come for us eventually, guess we were right. When are we leaving, Sir?"

"First of all, I'm not a sir; I'm a chief. Second, I'm not your savior, and I'm half-tempted to leave your asses where I found you. From now on I'm in charge. No more 'hanging back.' Are we all on the same page?"

The room was silent; the men in the back sat with their heads down. Walkens and Wilson just looked dazed, as though they had zero interest in the conversation. Brook stepped past them and looked at the men in the back.

"The chief just asked you a question! Are you going to give him an answer?" Brooks shouted.

The men in the back looked up, then back down again. Walkens and Wilson shuffled back against the wall.

"Let's go, Chief, there's nobody left alive up here; nothing worth saving," Brooks said, shouldering his rifle and walking toward the lounge doors.

"No wait! We're not bad guys ... everyone is just in shock. We thought everyone was gone. We're with you, Chief; whatever you need. Don't leave us," Bill said.

"Okay, well good then, but I'm going to need a spark of motivation out of you all if you want to get out of here. So everybody up off your asses, I want all of the supplies laid out in this hallway in twenty minutes and no holding back," Sean barked.

"What the hell are you waiting for? The chief just said get your shit and get it laid out in the hallway. Now *move!*" Brooks yelled.

The newly-found survivors jumped to their feet and disappeared into the living cells and started dragging gear into the hallway. Mr. Douglas and Swanson helped them organize it into piles. They had cases of MREs, several more cases of water, and close to four and a half cans of small arms ammunition. The men from the third floor were at least well stocked.

When all the gear had been organized, the men fell back out into the hallway. Sean was walking amongst the stacks of food and supplies taking notes. Their stores had grown but so had their numbers. The group now totaled twelve people. If he could organize them, it would give them a much better chance of getting off of the oil platform.

Sean put everyone to work. First they needed to clean out the area, since they couldn't live in this filth. Brad and Brooks organized working parties. They dragged the dead down to the second floor and pushed the bodies out office windows and into the still raging sea. They left the windows open, letting the sea air purge the smells of the primal stench from the building.

Everyone pitched in. It took the rest of the day, but by the end they had cleaned and organized the building. The Marines were slowly falling back into line seemingly happy to be back under leadership and working towards a goal. Brad posted guards in the first floor lounge and they put together a watch rotation. The building was secure.

8.

Brad found Sean sitting in one of the second floor offices looking out of the window towards the sea. The rain was still coming down hard but the winds had died down. It had been two days since they'd locked down the building. The area had been cleaned top to bottom and, other than the bullet holes and ripped down doors, most signs of the primals had been removed. Sean had organized them back into a fighting force, even if they didn't all agree on everything.

"So what are you thinking, Sean?"

"Trying to figure out how to get us out of this mess. I have been trying the phone; signal is good, but no answer. I guess the Colonel is done with us."

"Sean, the men are getting tired of all of the cleaning; they're getting anxious."

Sean turned in his chair and smiled at Brad. "Brad, how long have you been pushing troops?"

"Long enough I guess, why?"

"You should know then, all the yelling I have been doing about cleaning this shithole up wasn't about my OCD, it was about order. Think about it … If I had busted in here on day one and told those guys to suit up, we're going zombie hunting, they would have shut down on me. Instead I got them started on busy work for the last two days, so now they are so damn bored they can't wait to get back into the fight."

Brad smiled, shaking his head. He walked into the office, found a chair in the corner, and sat down. "Guess that's why you're the Chief. I hope it works."

"Brad, if we can't pull these guys back into a cohesive unit, we're all screwed. We need to keep them busy and tied down. Yeah, sure they are going to bitch, but the more work we toss at them, the more it keeps them focused on something else. Don't worry, it will all come together."

"So what's the plan then Chief? Where does this all go? How the hell we gonna get off this damn thing?"

"I don't know, man. We could get on that Blackhawk, try to assault an airfield and get us a fixed wing ... try and fly home. But sounds kind of John Wayne to me, too many moving parts to make it work. I'm starting to think our best bet may be to grab us one of the attack boats moored below. Take us awhile longer, but I think we could make it home."

"The bottom deck with the docks? How do you plan on getting us down there?"

"I've got some ideas; can you get the men together for me in the upstairs lounge in about thirty minutes? I think it's time to have a strategy session."

Brad gathered everyone in the upstairs lounge. It was a far sight from the room they had entered two days ago. All of the damaged and soiled furniture had been removed and tossed into the sea. Instead of the stench of primal, there was a strong scent of pine oil and bleach. All of the team had gathered around the room, sitting in chairs salvaged from the lower offices. The emergency lighting had been restored and gray daylight was coming in through a broken shatterproof window.

Sean entered the room and grabbed for a bottle of water sitting on a shelf. He opened the top and poured in a tube of instant coffee, shaking the bottle and taking a swig of the room temperature liquid. He walked across the room and glanced at the floor; it had been freshly mopped and the trash cans were empty. He smiled, knowing that his team was following his orders down to the most mundane detail. It was time. He sat in a chair across from them.

"Gentlemen ... and lady ... it's time we take back this platform. We need a way out of here and we can't do that unless we are in control of this facility. We have a helicopter but we can't fly it without fuel; there are ships below but we can't get to them. It's time to take back what is ours."

"Chief, how we gonna do that?" Ben asked.

"We are going to kill them all."

Sean explained his plan. Over the last two days, the primals outside had begun to detect the presence of the men inside the building. They had been slowly gathering outside the first floor doors. Every night they pounded on the steel fire doors, trying to gain entry. Brooks had found an entry way onto the building's roof, and they were able to look down onto the crowd outside the entrance.

The plan was simple. The Marines would go into the lounge, reinforce the doors, and make as much noise as possible, luring the mob to them. Sean, Brad, and Brooks would shoot them from their elevated position on the roof. The upside—they should be able to put them down and stay relatively safe; the downside—they would deplete most of their ammo for the sniper rifles.

Sean told the men to prepare themselves; they would start the purge as soon as it got dark and the creatures were most active. The men left the room excited—glad to be back on mission and ready to take back the platform.

9.

Brad was in the first floor lounge helping the Marines pile furniture against the doors. They had slid the heavy pool table against them and piled chairs (and anything else they could lift) on top of it. They didn't think the primals could breach the fire doors, but why take risks if they didn't have to? Swanson was getting the men into position. Sean had put the corporal in charge of the Marine privates, and she had excelled at the position.

"You ready, Swanson?"

"Yeah Sergeant, we got this, you just tell us when and we'll make a heck of a racket. You guys just make sure and kill all of them."

Brad pulled her aside, away from the other Marines. "It won't happen, but if they somehow breach, make sure you get all of your people pulled back into the hallway before you seal the second doors. I know you of all people understand that."

"Yeah, understood Sergeant; and you're right, that's not going to happen."

"Okay, we got a deal. I'm going to take Walkens up with me. When we're in position, I'll send him back down to indicate it's time to party."

Brad looked around the room one last time. The Marines had done well with the barricades; they had cut pipes to bang together as noise makers. He saw a large radio sitting on a bench.

"Hey, where did you all find that?"

Wilson grinned, holding up the old boom box. "I found this old piece of junk in the janitor's closet. Has a cassette tape in it, figured if the batteries work, we can turn it up as loud as it'll go. Worth a shot, right?"

"Good thinking Wilson! Alright Devil Dogs, if everyone is feeling hooah, hooah, I'm going to head up top and get ready to kick this thing off."

"Ooorah! Sergeant!" the Marines shouted.

"Damn, y'all are about as hard as woodpecker lips." Brad laughed as he made his way up to the roof being tailed by Walkens.

Brad found the ladder to the roof maintenance hatch and climbed his way to the platform that rested below the helipad. He found Brooks and Sean perched on an overlook. There were safety lines tied off to piping, and Brad clipped himself in. He approached Sean at the edge of the roof and took a knee.

"Okay Brad, I want you to engage the targets in front of the door. Keep an eye on those stairs leading to the helipad. We don't want them getting above us. Make sure nothing gets in. I'm going to take long shots of opportunity anywhere they pop up. Brooks is on the other side of the roof. He will clear out the storage deck and concentrate his fire on the stairs going down to the second deck."

"Okay, I think I can handle that," Brad said.

"And another thing ... be damn sure of what you are shooting at. We *are* on an oil rig; I don't want to light this thing up and become a crispy critter," Sean finished.

When everyone was in position, Brad yelled to Walken to get back downstairs and tell Swanson that it was 'go time'. They heard him running through the hallway below. Brad pulled his rifle into his shoulder and started searching the darkness. He took deep breaths to relax himself as he ran through his pre-combat checks.

The sun had just set; he could just make out a few figures walking the decks with his naked eye. His night vision was powered up and working perfectly. He pulled them down, and watched the deck light up into green and blacks. The rain was still coming down, but the lightning was far off and the winds had subsided.

Brad was sitting in a good firing position when he started hearing the clanging of bars and pounding against the walls downstairs. Then they heard a loud DONNNNNG! DONNNNNG! DONNNNNG! "What the hell is that?" Sean asked.

"I don't know, man, but the primals are waking up ... I see them climbing the stairs," Brooks called out.

The DONNNNNG! DONNNNNG! continued and was now joined by an electric guitar solo. Brad smiled. "Oh, shit! I think Wilson's boom box works; sounds like he's playing us some AC/DC tonight!"

They could just make out the lyrics of 'Hells Bells' as the first of the primals began moaning. Soon the platform was thundering with the sounds of primals and AC/DC.

"I'm rolling thunder, pouring rain"

"I have heavy contacts ... They're rushing up the steps. I won't be able to hold them all!" Brooks shouted.

"I'm coming on like a hurricane"

Brad heard the report of Brook's M14 rifle launching the heavy 7.62 rounds. The primals were charging down the walkway. Sean's rifle joined the chorus and Brad watched the numbers thin as the mass moved towards the doors. He pulled the rifle tight, and just before they got to the entrance, he took a deep breath and fired.

"I won't take no prisoners, won't spare no lives"

Brad watched one of the primals flinch and snap back, but another quickly took its place. He had been cautioned early by Sean to not 'double tap' and to stay away from the three-round burst. Ammo was now a precious commodity, so one shot/one kill was the rule for this hunt. Brad tried to calm his nerves and make every shot count.

He put his dot on another creature, pulled back on the trigger, and felt the recoil. The creature moved at the last second and the round impacted it high in the shoulder. Brad cursed himself for the miss. He closed his eyes tight and then relaxed his eye back on the scope. He found another target and put the dot at the base of its neck, pulled the trigger, and watched it drop.

"I got my bell I'm gonna take you to Hell; I'm gonna get ya Satan get ya"

They were now massed heavily on the doors, pounding and screaming. Brad was picking out targets and firing calmly as he tried to make every round count. Sean's and Brooks' rifles barked in the target-rich environment. Brass was piling up around all of them. Brad reached into his pack for a fresh magazine, let the bolt go forward, and took up aim again.

He found one that was pulling hard on the door's handle, and dropped him quickly. He searched for a new target and saw motion in his peripheral vision. A group of them were now charging up the stairs to the helipad. He switched his position and turned, firing rapidly to stop the creatures' crude attempts at a flanking maneuver. He knocked down the leaders who fell backwards, taking the others with them.

"Hell's bells, you got me ringing, Hell's bells"

Brad brought his attention back to the door. The primals had forced a corner of the door back and were pulling on it. There was a massive pile of dead in front of the entrance that partially prevented them from being able to pull it open. Brad saw sparks below that indicated the Marines were now firing through the door, joining the fight.

"I'll give you black sensations up and down your spine"

The mass withered. Sean's rifle went silent; soon after Brooks halted as well. Brad searched and scanned the pile below. Sean sounded off that his sector was clear, and Brooks followed suit. Brad made another pass and was about to speak when he saw movement at a corner. He focused his vision and saw the Alpha leader they had spotted days earlier on the platform. Brad tried to pick up a sight picture just as the Alpha disappeared.

"I'm clear but I think one got away!" Brad shouted.

Sean made his way to Brad's position. "What do you mean ... got away?"

"I don't know Sean, it's like he ... like he fell back ... he ... ahh ... retreated," Brad sputtered in disbelief.

"What? They don't do that. These things are lemmings; they always rush to their death."

"I'm telling you Chief, it was the big leader from a few days ago! He was watching from around that corner right there. Just as I got a bead on him, he tucked and disappeared."

"Shit, well if that's true, it makes things a bit more interesting." Sean paused for a moment. "Okay, nothing we can do about it now. Let's get downstairs and check on the kids," he said as he started packing up his gear.

10.

Brad and Sean made the walk downstairs together in search of the Marines. They found them in the lounge. They were cheering and patting each other on the back. This was the first victory they had achieved against the primals.

"We whooped them good, Chief," Walkens called out.

"Calm down hero, we just shot a bunch a fish in a barrel, but yeah, you all did well."

"Nahh Chief, you don't understand; those things chased our asses all the way out of Afghanistan. We always been on the run from them. This is the first time we kicked their asses."

The Marines in the room burst into cheers.

"What's next Chief, we going to assault the next deck?" Swanson asked.

"Alright, everyone calm down. You guys kicked ass, I get that, and yeah, we took back this deck … maybe. Let's wait till first light. Once the sun comes up we'll run some recons and make sure we secured the deck," Sean said.

"Screw that, Chief, let's do it now!" Wilson yelled.

Brooks walked out of the hallway and took a seat on the pool table stacked against the doors. "Y'all do realize we only dropped about seventy-five to a hundred of those things just now, don't ya? From what I understand there were five hundred stationed here. Yeah, maybe the rest were able to evacuate, but I think I'd rather wait until daylight to figure that out," he said.

"Okay, okay, so what we going to do till tomorrow, I'm all ramped up," Walkens asked.

"Uhhh, I got an idea," Tony the civilian said as he walked into the room from the hallway.

"You do, huh?" Sean asked.

Tony reached into a small knapsack and pulled out a full bottle of bourbon. "How 'bout a bit of Kentucky windage to celebrate and calm our nerves, Chief?"

"Shit," Sean said, looking at the bottle. Then he looked around the room and saw the men's faces light up. "Well, seein' as you got one bottle to split twelve ways, I'd say what the hell, break out some glasses. And Tony, you better not be sneaking open another bottle. When this one's gone, that's it."

The men clamored to pull down glasses from a cabinet, and they grouped around Tony, slapping him on the back as he careful divided the precious liquid between them. Brad hesitated, then walked towards the corner of the room to sit in a chair.

"Shoot, get over here and get your share, Army," Swanson called out.

Brad started to say no, until the rest of the Marines cheered for him to join in. He grinned and walked across the room to take a cup. He sniffed the liquid; Tony apparently was not a connoisseur of fine bourbons. Brad took a sip of the brown stuff and felt it burn as it went down. He made a face, which again caused the men to cheer.

Brad smiled back at the men and steadied the glass, then picked up his gear with his free hand. He turned and moved into the hallway, walking slowly on the clean vinyl tile. He walked until he found an office with intact furniture and moved in, dumping his gear to the floor with a thud. The office held a sofa and a large steel desk with an old, high back chair behind it.

He went behind the desk and took a seat in the chair. Unbuckling holsters, he placed his M9 and S&W Sigma pistols on the desk, then leaned back and put up his feet. He took another sip of the whiskey and felt the burn, this time enjoying it a bit more. He pulled a water bottle from his cargo pocket and added water to the glass. Not so much to water it down, but to make it last just a bit longer.

Brad could hear the men joking in the lounge; the mood lifted with the sudden feelings of security now that the deck was presumed clear. Brad looked over his shoulder, opened the blinds behind him, and some light spilled into the room. Looking out, he was surprised to see the rains had finally stopped and he could see the moon.

"Looks like the weather finally broke," Swanson said, breaking the silence.

Brad looked up and saw her standing in the doorway. "Yeah, looking that way. What can I help you with, Corporal?"

"Please, call me Chelsea," she answered.

"Okay ... Chelsea ... What's up?"

"Mind if I take a seat?" she asked as she looked at the sofa across the room from Brad.

"Sure, take a load off," he answered, lifting his glass in a mock salute.

Chelsea leaned her rifle against the wall, plopped onto the sofa, leaned back and took a sip from her half empty glass before making a foul face.

"Here, add some water, it mellows it a bit," Brad said, tossing her the water bottle.

Chelsea smiled and filled her glass back to the top with water, then took another sip, making the same face. "I don't think it helped much. I'd kill for a Coke right now."

"So what brings you to my office, Chelsea?' Brad asked just before he took another sip of his bourbon.

"Just looking for some company," she smiled back.

"What, the privates don't entertain you?" Brad chuckled.

"Yeah, turns out that crude jokes and ball scratching get old after a while," she laughed.

"Let me ask you Chelsea, how did you find your way onto this rig? Why weren't you sent back to the States?"

"The States, I wish ... I mean, what's left of them, anyway. I haven't heard anything from them in weeks. After the fall, this is where we were dropped. But it's still better than on the ground. We were cornered against the walls of the airfield and we had been holding up for days hiding in the bunkers. With the armor, we were holding the lines, doing the best we could. Some officers were trying to get everyone out, but there weren't enough planes on the ground to move everyone."

"I'd heard they recalled everyone back to the States and closed the bases. My unit never got a warning; my company was lost in the field. At least you had the evac order," Brad said.

"Oh, they tried, I'll give them that ... the first days of the evacuation were impressive; huge airlift flights leaving the ground and landing every few minutes. The Cobras and Apaches were tearing up wave after wave of primals, trying to cover the withdrawal. After a couple of days, the flights dwindled with the fuel supplies. Combat troops and those with special skills were getting priority to be sent back to the States. I was in a maintenance unit and kept getting passed over.

"Eventually, they asked for techs and mechanical types to volunteer to help get these rigs online as staging areas. Our commander jumped at the chance to get us out of that place. A Chinook helicopter picked up my team and dropped us here. It was good duty, considering ... and they said once the Navy ship was replenished they would be getting us home."

"Yeah, shitty luck I guess ... what'd you know about the attacks? How did we lose Leatherneck? All that muscle and advanced warning, I'd figure they would hold forever."

Chelsea took a long pull on her glass and spoke quietly, "We heard the rumors and were briefed about the 'zombie' attacks, or whatever they were, but nobody believed it. The camp was put on lock down, and nobody was allowed in or out. We had a hundred percent up on the walls but nothing happened. We joked about it, but folks were getting pissed off about pulling twelve hour shifts out on the wire.

"We heard stories of camps in the north getting overrun and about Bagram falling. Comms started failing, we lost Internet access ... then the sirens blared in the middle of the second night. At first they came in ones and twos. Even though we were warned, the sergeants of the guard still hesitated; they didn't want to shoot unarmed civilians. But that didn't last long. Not after we saw the damage they could do.

"Eventually our gate was hit by a wave of thousands. The machine guns fired until their barrels warped. Airstrikes and gunships pounded them. It didn't take long before the base was surrounded and they were in so close that we couldn't get effective support from the artillery guns. The main gates fell; they swarmed and pushed in.

"The armor saved us; the Bradleys and Abrams tanks rushed forward and plugged the break in the wall. We thought we stopped them. The mass had been beaten back, their numbers dwindled, but we screwed up. It was the 'No man gets left behind' and the whole 'brothers in arms' thing that screwed us."

"What do you mean by that?" Brad asked.

"We didn't understand then how it spread. Some of our guys were really kicking the shit out of those things. But they got scratched and bit. Their buddies carried them back to base and took them to the medics. Hell, we didn't know they would all turn; nobody told us that part. The hospital fell; units were torn apart from the inside. Segregation orders for the wounded finally came down, but too much damage had already been done.

"It was bad. We were pulled back and we fortified the airfield in final defensive positions. The armor formed a wall of steel and the Air Force dropped in ammo and supplies around the clock. Our guys on the line were holding them back, but they just kept coming. They are attracted to noise, you know … so the more we fought, the more were drawn in; a never-ending loop. When the captain told us we had been tasked to the oil rigs, I felt such relief to be leaving. Everyone knew they were fighting a losing battle."

"What happened to the guys on the ground? Did you hear anything from them?" Brad asked.

"I don't know. We left for the rig seven days after the first attack, and we stopped getting reports from the airfield on day ten. Maybe they all got out."

"Yeah, I'm sure they all got out," Brad said slowly.

"Are we ever getting off of this platform, Army?"

"You know what, call me Brad, and yeah, I think we will. We didn't last this long to die out at sea. Why don't you get some rest, Chelsea? It's going to be a long day tomorrow."

"Okay. Brad? Thanks for listening, I appreciate it. Goodnight," she said, placing the empty glass on the desk and walking from the room.

Brad drained the rest of his glass and left it on the desk next to Chelsea's. He stood to stretch out the cramps and was surprised at the whiskey's effect on him. His tolerance must have slipped quite a bit after all of those months in the desert. Taking his own advice, he picked up his weapons and gear, then made his way to the third floor sleeping quarters.

11.

The morning came with a brightness that Brad had forgotten existed in this part of the world. He had gotten used to the cool, long rainy days and cloudy skies. It was all they had seen since they'd arrived on the platform. Now the sun was shining brightly through his cell's windows. The steel roof above him was radiating the heat.

He sat up in his bunk and rested his feet on the cool tile floor. The living cell he now occupied was far from luxurious, but it beat the hell out of anything he had stayed in since the first of the attacks. There wasn't much to it; a large wardrobe locker and a desk sat on the wall opposite his tiny bunk. His gear was piled in front of him, taking up much of the floor space.

Brad heard a commotion in the hall. He stood, stretching and yawning, then pulled on a pair of MultiCam trousers before he opened the door and walked out. The men were moving about, strapping on their armor and prepping their weapons.

"What's going on guys?" Brad asked.

"We're going outside. Chief said we're going to take back the top deck. Good shit, right Sergeant?" Private Craig quickly answered.

Brad moved across the hall and into the lounge. He found Brooks drinking down a bottle of instant coffee.

"You have any more of that?"

"Sure, help yourself," Brooks answered, sliding a couple of packets of the instant coffee across the table.

Brad twisted the cap off a bottle of water and emptied the packets in. Shaking the bottle, he watched the liquid change color. "So the guys tell me we're moving outside today."

"Yup. Chief wants the deck secured as soon as possible; with the sun shining bright it's the best time to take advantage of the momentum we built last night."

Brad took a swig of the bitter, barely warm coffee just as Sean walked in the door from downstairs.

"Good morning sunshine! I see someone decide to sleep in today," Sean said, moving to take a seat at the table. "I assume Brooks filled you in on this morning's mission?"

Brad nodded as he yawned and took another long sip from the bottle.

"You think you're up to taking Swanson and a couple of the new guys out on your own? Brooks and I will pull the other two along. Probably best to leave the fly boys and civilians to hold the fort."

"Works for me; better if we move as fire teams out on the deck anyhow. When do you want to get started?"

"Get your stuff together. We all meet below in fifteen." Sean said, smiling.

Brad tossed his empty bottle into the trash can and moved back to his cell to prep his gear. The Marines were up, slapping each other on the backs and getting fired up for today's operation. The bravado and camaraderie gave Brad flashbacks to a time before all of this shit—back to a time when he was running patrols with his own men. When Brad would get the pre-mission jitters and share in the excitement of going out.

Brad suited up and stepped into the hall just as the last of the men were making their way down the stairs. He found them assembled in the first floor lounge around the pool table. Sean had a fire emergency escape map of the platform laid out on the table. He had the three exits to the lower decks circled in red, and big X's drawn through the doorways leading into the other two structures.

Sean looked across the table at Swanson and the group of Marines. "We're going to sweep and clear the outside. Corporal, I want you to pick two of your Marines and join Sergeant Thompson," Sean said.

"No problem, Chief," she quickly replied back. "Wilson? You and Craig are with me."

"Okay good. Captain, I want you and the civilians to hold this position. Nobody gets in or out while we are outside. Be ready to open the doors in a hurry."

"Understood, Chief," Bradley answered.

"Brooks and I will form the second fire team with you two then," Sean said, pointing across at Walkens and Nelson, who nodded back in acknowledgement. "Gentleman, this is going to take a while but we're not going to be rushed. Time is one thing we have plenty of."

Sean broke down the rest of the plan to secure the third deck. They needed to first barricade the main stairway going down to the second deck. Then they would cut the remaining two ladders that led below to ensure that nothing could sneak up them. When they were sure that all ingress and egress routes were secured, they would work on clearing the final two structures.

"If everything goes as planned, maybe we'll have lights and running water tonight," Sean joked. "Let's gear up and be ready to step out in five mikes."

***

Brad was stacked against the exit door, looking at his team. "Let keep this simple, guys. Maintain eye contact with one another and cover your sectors. Don't go pointing your weapons at your buddies. If we make contact, listen to the sound of my voice, I'll tell you where I want you. Too easy, right?"

"Too easy, Sergeant, we got this," Swanson answered for the others.

Brad looked up and nodded to Brooks, who unlocked the doors. Bill and Tony helped him push hard on the doors to ease the pile of broken and twisted bodies piled against it from the previous night's battle. The right side opened just enough to allow the teams to exit. Brooks moved out with his team in tow and cut right; Brad, moving at the same time, took his team to the left.

Once outside, Brad moved just beyond the blind corner where he had been surprised by the giant primal days earlier and took a knee. The walkway was covered with corpses and the smell was horrible. They had been living with it for weeks now, so it didn't hit him as hard as it had in the past. Swanson took a knee across from him, the two Marines just behind and facing in the opposite direction.

Sean's team moved down the walkway towards the helipad stairs. Brad waited for them to get to their location and set in position. He sent Swanson and Wilson forward and then followed behind with Craig. Each team moved in concert, leapfrogging each other so that at all times six of the eight fighters were covering while two moved. Moving slowly, they overlapped their sectors, bounding and covering each other's movements, until they reached the storage deck.

Brad's team was on line just off the walkway looking down the right side of the storage deck. Sean's group had taken up positions to the left. The deck appeared clear other than some tossed-about crates and torn tarps flapping in the subtle ocean breeze. The sun was in full effect, heating everything up. Brad could see bodies lying on the ground in various states of decay, but so far there was no movement.

Brad looked to Sean, who pointed at his own shirt collar indicating he wanted Brad to move to his position. He told Swanson to take charge and keep her eyes on the surroundings, then ran at a low hunch to Sean's position and took a knee.

"What's up boss?" he asked.

"Okay, let's clear this deck in line. Eyes on everyone at all times. It's pretty hot and bright out here so I don't suspect we have any hiders, but let's not take any chances. If anything, we can at least work out the kinks with the new guys. You take the right side, we got left, don't get in front of us, keep the firing lanes open, and we'll meet at the stairway," Sean whispered.

"Got it, Chief," Brad answered and turned to return to his group.

Brad's people moved slowly, clearing every corner and obstacle as they moved on line with each other. The deck held pallet after pallet of MREs, cases of water, ammunition, and fifty-gallon barrels of different assortments of fuel. Most of the heavy stacks appeared undamaged. The most they found was sheathes of ripped plastic, flapping from crates, that had probably been blown loose in the storm.

They stepped over downed bodies while taking note of the weapons on the ground. Slowly they navigated the piles until the stairway came into view. Pallets and crates had been hastily pushed in front of the stairs in a worthy, although unsuccessful, attempt to barricade the entrance. The stairs opened up to a double-wide mouth, reminding Brad of the entrances to a subway tunnel.

Brad's group found cover to the right of the stairs just as Sean's team was dropping into position on the left. Sean signaled for Brad to get eyes on the target while Brooks and one of his Marines crept forward toward the barricade. After several tense minutes, Brooks came to his feet and indicated the area was secure.

Brad brought his team forward and they moved to the stairs to gather near Sean. Sean quickly put them to work re-enforcing the barricade. The Marines dropped cases of spare parts and anything else they could lift into the stairwell until it was completely congested. It wouldn't keep out a raging mob, but they also wouldn't be able to break through without notice. Before moving on, Sean reached into his dump sack and handed Brad a handful of ties and some rubber wedges he had prepared earlier.

"We are going to move out along the walkway toward the support buildings, same as before. If you come up on any entrances to the buildings, don't worry about clearing them. Just secure the doors as best you can, zip tie the latches, and pile shit against them or wedge these blocks into the doors. When the deck is secured we'll begin moving into the structures," Sean said.

Brad nodded his understanding and they moved out just as before. Brad's team moved down the long walkway leading to the first of two support buildings. "That's the power station," Swanson whispered to Brad.

Brad just nodded in acknowledgement as they continued to move forward, covering Sean's team's movements as they covered his. Brad's team was skirting the seaside railing while Sean's team was looking into the platform on the other side of the walkway. Wilson raised his hand and pointed at the tip of a ladder that reached over the side of the platform from the lower deck.

Brad approached the ladder and looked down; he could see the empty deck below. He pulled a heavy wrench from his pack. The wrench fit the ladder bolts perfectly just as Tony had told them it would. With some heavy pulling and kicking, the first bolt broke its lock and started turning. They hadn't ever seen a primal climb a vertical ladder, but he would sleep better knowing that the ladders were gone. After some heavy turning, all of the bolts had been removed and Brad kicked the ladder. It fell free and tumbled to the bottom deck with a loud clatter.

Brad waved Sean's team forward and they moved to the power station where they found the doors hanging open. Brad peeked inside and could see the open engineering spaces. The one-story building's large open bay appeared to be empty, so they closed the door and sealed it shut as best they could. Moving forward, they watched as Sean's team removed the second ladder and secured the doors of the controls building.

They gathered in shade near the open walkway in front of the power station. Brad dropped to the ground and drank from a bottle. He guzzled it halfway down before tossing the other half to Sean, who finished it before sticking the empty in his pocket. It had only taken two hours to clear the deck, but those two hours in the sun had exhausted them.

Sean sent two of the Marines back to inform the others that the decks were clear and to begin the process of removing the dead. The rest of them would get to work on clearing the two remaining buildings. It had already been a long day, but it was far from over.

12.

The rest of the team stacked up on the door to the power station. Brad pulled the wedge from under the door, and at the count of three he yanked it open. They held a small firing line just outside the entrance, waiting for a rush of primals that never came. After some uncomfortable minutes, Brad moved in front of the doorway and cut inside, with Brooks close behind him.

They found themselves in a large, steel-clad building with one long open bay. The room was dark, hot, and stank of burnt oil and weld dust. There was a small workspace in the corner with an instrument panel and a bank of switches. The far wall was lined with huge generators. The opposing wall held a number of machines and tool and die equipment. Brad and Brooks carefully walked the room and searched the shadows.

"Room's clear," Brooks called out.

The rest of the team entered the building and began to look around. Sean went to the workspace and searched through piles of papers and engineering drawings, but found nothing useful. "Swanson, what do you need to get the lights back on?" he asked.

"I'll need some help getting fuel drums swapped out, and then it should be as simple as kicking the gennies back up and bringing the breakers online. Bill and Tony would be a lot of help. They *are* the platform engineers, so this is their expertise."

"Very well. Take Wilson and Craig back to the lounge and grab Bill and Tony. Let's get this place powered up," Sean said.

He walked outside and away from the building, followed by Brooks and Brad. They stood against the railing looking down at the sea. The seas were still choppy but the clouds had all but disappeared. Looking down, they could see that a number of the vessels that had been there earlier were now gone; they'd probably been destroyed from being smashed against the platform's pylons in the storm, or came loose from their moorings and drifted away.

A large Pakistani-flagged fast attack craft and another smaller military ship still sat tied side by side below them. The smaller of the military ships showed a great deal of hull damage, but the other looked to be in good condition. Farther off, a large fishing boat sat, drifting away from the platform but still connected by a long length of stretched heavy rope. There was no sign of life on any of the ships; they looked dead in the water.

"What are your thoughts on the FAC?" Sean asked Brooks.

"Hmmm, looks like a MRTP-33. Hull looks okay from here, but I'd have to get in the water to really check it out. I don't know; guess if we followed the coastline we'd be okay. We could always trade up later," Brooks answered.

"You really thinking on driving that thing eight thousand miles?" Brad asked, looking to Sean.

"Well, sailing actually. Those ships are pretty reliable; would make a good platform for raiding ports as we make our way home. Nothing says we can't find a better method along the way, though."

"Okay, but how the hell are we going to get all the way down there?" Brad asked.

"Guess we fight our way down," Sean replied.

Tony and Bill came up behind the trio talking at the rail. Tony looked down at the ship. "Chief, I didn't mean to listen in but we don't have to take the lower decks at all."

"How's that, Tony? You care to explain?"

"Well shit, Chief, if you plan on taking that there boat, you would have to resupply it with the crane anyhow; I mean to lower down fuel and such. The crane and operator's station are up here. I could drop you and your men right on top of that thing without ever going downstairs."

"Son of a bitch, now that's a good idea, Tony!"

"Yeah, you'd still have to get down there and secure it though—make sure none of them things are on board and keep them from jumping on it from the docks. I figure you could sneak on, untie it, and then attach it to one of the pylons farther out. That should keep them off ya."

"That's good thinking, Tony. How are we coming with the power?"

"Should be on shortly, Chief. The kids are bringing over more fuel right now, so guess I should get back over there."

"Good work. And thanks, Tony. Let me know if you have any problems."

Bill and Tony turned to walk away just as the Marines rounded the corner with a cart full of fuel drums headed to the power station.

"Let's keep that in mind for a while. I figure it's time to get back to work. We need to clear the control building before sunset ... I don't expect much trouble, the doors were swung open and the windows were broken out when I sealed it up earlier," Sean said.

They gathered up and walked past the power station. Brad peeked in the door and saw a flurry of activity. The Marines were working hard, refueling the power plants. "I think we can handle this on our own, guys," Sean said. Brooks and Brad nodded in agreement. They had been through far worse without the help of anyone, Brad thought to himself.

The men finished the walk to the one-story steel building. There was a large tower, not unlike an air traffic control tower, only on a much smaller scale. The tower extended a good seventy-five feet into the air and appeared to be topped by an observation bubble. A radio antenna extended another hundred feet above that.

Sean and his men stood near the door. As they had discovered earlier, there were several large windows in the face of this building at shoulder height. The windows were all smashed and Brad could easily see inside. The sun was in the perfect location, and light was filling most of the structure. Sean readied his MP5 as Brooks kicked the wedge from the bottom of the door. Sean touched the handle and the door swung open.

They surrounded the entrance in a half-circle, listening and waiting for anything or anyone. After a few minutes, Brooks swept into the room and cut left. Brad moved in and to the right, closely followed by Sean. The men had become very good at working together. Very little verbal or hand communication was required with the trio; they had become a tight cohesive force.

Brooks positioned himself at the end of the room at the entrance to the next doorway. The team stacked up and cleared their way through the entire first floor. They found offices filled with banks of computers and control panels that appeared to run the rig's drilling equipment and life support systems. Fortunately, no primals or bodies were found inside. This building must have had early warning, or was possibly unoccupied during the attacks.

They found a locked hatch to the observation tower but waited before breeching it. Satisfied that the rest of the building was clear, they relaxed their posture and began looking around. Brad found a large control panel labeled 'desalinization'. He pointed it out to Sean, who smiled and said he hoped it was still operational.

"Damn, between the systems in this room and the pallets of food and water on the decks, we could make a home here for quite a while." Brooks said.

"Sure as hell seems that way. Let's just hope all this shit works," Sean said.

As if on cue, they heard a rumble from the power station. The noise quickly evened out to a purr, and suddenly the lights in the control room popped on. Several of the control panels started lighting up and the computers began to beep and boot up. The men smiled at each other as they examined the gauges and dials.

Brad looked back at the desalinization panel; the status lights quickly went from flashing red to solid green. The digital gauge on the fresh water tanks showed full. Another indicated that the boilers were back online and water pressure was nominal.

"Hell yeah! Look at this," Brad said, pointing at the gauges.

"Hot showers tonight guys," Brooks laughed.

The celebration was short-lived, however, as the sounds of gunfire and screams erupted from outside.

"What the fuck is that? Move to contact, let's go!" Sean yelled.

Brooks quickly put his game face back on and stepped out at a quick trot towards the source of the firing. Brad was right behind him, moving parallel to Sean. The intensity of the firing had quickened and was now mixed with the sounds of primal moans. Brooks turned a corner and his MP5 barked. He didn't stop; he kept moving forward, keeping the weapon at his eye, and firing controlled shots as he moved.

Brad sped to keep up. He had his own weapon at the ready as he saw a mass of figures at the end of the walkway near the cranes. Sean's weapon began to fire next to him. Brad searched for targets, trying to distinguish friend from foe.

He finally saw one of the Marines on his back, struggling. A primal was bent over him, clawing and chewing frantically. Brad held his breath and took careful aim, then fired two rounds. His first shots landed in the primal's hip, spinning the primal away from the Marine. Brad fired again, connecting with its upper chest and head. The beast arched backwards before falling slack against the deck.

Brad pivoted in search of more targets while leaving his eye against his optics. He scanned from left to right. The firing stopped and was replaced by the screaming of the man still on the ground. It was Ben Walkens, one of the Marines who had been assisting with the cleanup. Brooks ran quickly to his side and dropped down, cutting away Ben's body armor and clothing.

Walkens had scratches all over his face, and deep cuts and chunks of flesh missing from his left shoulder and arm. Brooks pulled a small bottle of alcohol from his aid bag and dumped it all over the Marine's face and onto his wounded arm, then grabbed a gauze pad and began scrubbing the wounds. Walkens screamed frantically in pain. Nelson had moved forward and was trying to hold the injured man so Brooks could work. Brooks gave Walkens a dose of morphine, then stood and walked away. Sean approached him.

"How's it look?" Sean asked.

"You know damn well how it looks, Chief. He's cut wide the fuck open and you know what that means. I poured as much alcohol as I had in the wounds and cleaned them as best I could. Who the fuck knows? Maybe it will kill the infection. How the fuck did this happen?" Brooks stood, shaking his head. "Chief, I need a minute," he said with deep frustration in his voice.

Brooks turned and walked away from the scene. Sean approached Walkens, still on the ground and a bit more calm with the morphine in his system. Nelson was sitting next to him, applying a pressure dressing to his arm. Brad was walking among the dead primals, double checking that they were terminated.

"How you feeling, pal?" Sean asked Walkens.

"I'm gonna turn into one of those things, ain't I, Chief?"

"We don't know that. Brooks is a good medic. Let's just wait and see, okay buddy?"

"Just don't let me turn into one of these things, Chief," Walkens pleaded.

"Just relax; we're going to take good care of you." Sean reached into Brooks' aid bag and gave Walkens another dose of the morphine. Walkens' gaze faded and he looked away, talking to himself.

Sean looked back to Nelson. "What the hell happened, Nelson?"

"Me and Ben ... we was moving things ... clearing the deck. We heard the power kick on ... we was smiling and ... joking about hot food tonight." Nelson's voice started to break as he looked down at his friend. The rest of the men had arrived at the scene and started to gather.

"It's okay, Nelson. Just tell me where these things came from," Sean said softly.

"From there, Chief." Nelson pointed to a caged lift.

"How the hell? The lift was secured; it was in the lockout position. Bill and Tony said they checked it," Sean exclaimed.

"That's right, Chief, the engage bar was set to lockout," Bill confirmed.

"I don't know, Chief, we was standing right here. We heard the lift click; then the light turned green and it started to rise. Them things must have engaged it and pressed the operate button," Nelson said.

Just then they heard the lift click again; the green light switched from green to red, and it started to drop into the lower deck.

"What the fuck!" Sean yelled. Brad and Sean ran forward, weapons at the ready, watching the lift drop. "Shut that thing down!" Sean yelled to Bill.

Bill ran to a control box and started digging through wires. "The breaker is below; I can kill it from here though ... I just gotta find and disconnect the ground." The lift finished its move to the lower deck, making a loud *clunk*. The red light went out. The lift made another loud *clunk*, the light turned green, and it started to move up again.

"Any time now Bill!" Sean yelled.

"I'm working on it Chief!"

Tony ran forward, fire axe in his hands, and shoved Bill out of the way. He swung the axe and severed half of the bundle. The lift still moved. Tony quickly adjusted his feet and swung hard again, severing the bundle in a bright spray of sparks. The lift hung dead with a short six inches of the top extending above the deck. The green light went out.

Brad let out a sigh of relief just as the primals in the lift began to moan. Brad stepped forward angrily and put his rifle into the small gap between the lift and the deck, ready to engage.

"Hold your fire!" Sean yelled.

"What?" Brad said, looking back.

"Save your ammo, they can't get up here and we don't want to rupture anything that will burn down there with wild shots," Sean answered.

Brad nodded back, but kept a nervous eye on the lift, trying to see the monsters' faces hiding in the shadows.

Sean turned back to Tony. "How the hell did the lift come up if it was locked out?" Sean asked.

"Someone ... or some*thing* ... had to have toggled the override below and pressed the lift button!" Tony stuttered.

"What the fuck? They're pushing buttons now?" Sean asked.

"It's the only way. Chief, you saw them call it back down! Those things are getting smarter," Tony gasped.

"Okay, are there any more lifts?"

"No Chief, this is the only one."

"Okay, listen up. Tony? Clean up that mess; I don't want those cut wires starting a fire. Swanson? You and Bill back to the power house; get this place online and get the water running. Craig? You and Wilson keep your eyes on this lift. I want the two of you patrolling between here and the stairway. The rest of you help me get Ben back to the lounge," Sean barked. "Any questions? No? Good, move out!"

13.

Ben's arms had been restrained and his legs bound together, but his head and torso were still free. They'd retrieved a mattress from one of the beds upstairs and laid him out on the lounge pool table to try and make him more comfortable. Sean was standing next to Ben, monitoring his breathing and heart rate. Nelson was asleep on the sofa. The officers had gone back outside to supervise the cleanup and security of the deck.

They'd hoped that the quick treatment of the wounds would save Ben but, as the clock ticked, they watched the infection take hold. The fever hit and Ben began to sweat profusely. The wounds turned dark then began streaking. Ben was coherent at first but as panic set in they gave him more morphine to relax. He slowly fell asleep, fading in and out of coherence.

"I'm thirsty, Chief," Ben's weakened voice rasped. He had been slipping in and out of consciousness, probably from the fever, but also the morphine.

"Here you go, buddy," Sean said, putting a bottle to Ben's lips.

Ben eagerly drank from the bottle before coughing and putting his head back down.

"Did the medicine work, Chief? Am I going to be okay?" he asked.

Sean looked down at Ben's battered face. The scratches had begun to turn a deep purple, even though Brooks had soaked them with alcohol and packed antibiotic cream into them. The infection had still taken hold. Ben's temperature had been rising at least one degree every thirty minutes. Sean looked across the room to Brooks, who was sorting through a box of medical supplies that had been scavenged from the platform's infirmary.

"Yeah, you're going to be fine. You just need some rest, okay?" Sean lied.

"Okay Chief," Ben answered before turning his head to the side and closing his eyes.

Feeling Sean's stare, Brooks took his attention from the box and frowned at Sean before shaking his head. Brooks went back to his task of sorting through the box, pulling items and stuffing them into his aid bag. Sean turned his attention back to the Marine, adjusting his sheets and trying to make him more comfortable.

Quickly Ben turned his head back towards him and struggled to sit up. "Chief!"

"Whoa relax, son. What is it, Ben?" Sean asked.

"Chief, please make sure I don't turn into one of those things, please, Chief."

"Don't worry buddy, we're going to take great care of you. Just get some rest now."

Ben relaxed and once again turned his head to the side and closed his eyes.

"Brad, can you take over? I need to get some air," Sean asked.

"Sure, I got it, Chief," Brad said, leaving his place at the back of the lounge.

Brad looked Ben over. Ben was unconscious now and sweating profusely. The scratches on his face were darkening, the deep purple outline spreading. The wounds on his arm had been covered, but dark red and blue lines streaked up from the bandaged limb. It was obvious that Ben was now infected. There would be no saving him.

Sean walked over to Brooks and whispered something to him before he left the room.

"It's too bad, bro," Brad said as he used a damp cloth to cool Ben's forehead.

"Too bad my ass! This was completely avoidable," Brooks said. "No excuse for us losing this kid."

"It is what it is, Brooks. We have to just keep moving forward," Brad replied flatly.

Brooks shook his head, then pulled a large syringe from his aid bag and a couple of unmarked glass bottles. He drew the fluid from both bottles into the syringe and injected it into a vein on Ben's good arm. He then secured the syringe in an empty water bottle before tossing it.

"Can you stay with him, Brad? I'm going to give his buddies an opportunity to say good bye; it won't be long now ... Be careful, I just gave him a dose big enough to kill a horse, but who knows how the virus works," Brooks said.

Brad nodded as Brooks left the room. He put his hand on Ben's chest and felt his labored breathing. It had been almost three hours since he had been attacked.

Brad heard the door swing open behind him. Swanson entered the room with Wilson and Craig. They were shaken but tried to hide it. There were no tears. The weeks of constant death and attacks had desensitized them to the agony of losing a friend.

"How is he?" Swanson asked.

"He only has a short time left. We gave him an overdose of diamorphine. He won't wake up," Brad answered.

"Good, he deserves to die a Marine and not as one of those things," Wilson said.

Brad felt the movement of Ben's chest stop; he slipped a hand to his wrist and couldn't find a pulse. Cautiously they all stepped back from the table and waited for the reboot.

Brooks and Sean came into the room and joined them around the table. Wilson woke up from his nap and sat up, feeling the somberness of the room. Brad shook his head at Sean and Brooks. Brooks came forward and also checked Ben for a pulse. When he failed to find one he held his hand to Ben's chest, then shook his head and moved back against the wall.

Sean came forward and removed Ben's dog tags. He handed them to Swanson.

"This is what happens when we fuck up. We got lazy, we assumed the deck was secure, and we didn't pay attention to the small details. This doesn't happen again. Get your friend cleaned up and prepare him for burial. Our work day isn't finished yet," Sean said.

Sean placed his hand on Ben's chest for a moment, then pulled the sheet gently over his head before stepping away and walking outside. After stopping to pat the sheet, Brad and Brooks followed Sean through the door.

14.

Brooks and Brad followed Sean back to the control room, and found him standing below the hatch to the observation tower. The hatch dogs were securely in place, but there didn't appear to be any physical lock to prevent them from opening it. Sean looked over to Brooks and nodded. Brooks raised his weapon and pointed at the hatch.

Sean carefully climbed the ladder to the top and began to un-dog the latches. They each freely opened with a slight metallic clang. The final latch clanged free and Sean looked back at Brooks and again nodded. He bent his legs and shoved the hatch up, throwing it open until it locked into place, then dropped back down the ladder and moved to the side to give Brooks a clear shot.

Brooks kept his weapon pointed at the now open compartment, trying to see inside. After a few tense moments, Sean drew his sidearm and again climbed the ladder. When he reached the top, he disappeared into the tube that led to the compartment. There was a large crash and a bang. The sound echoed down into the space below.

Brooks quickly jumped forward, grabbed the ladder and began to climb.

"Calm down ... It's okay ... Dammit ... I just banged my head. I'm fine, guys." Sean yelled down.

Brooks looked down at Brad still standing on the deck. Brad tried to hold back but finally lost it and burst into laughter. Brooks couldn't contain himself and gave out a large belly laugh.

"Glad you assholes think that's funny, now get up here!" Sean yelled down the ladder.

They found themselves in a small square room. The walls angled up on each side and were topped with large tinted-glass windows. The wall was cased with a desk and workspace, which was topped with an assortment of radios and computers. Located high in the air just above the height of the helicopter pad, they had an expansive view of the platform.

"Do you know how to use this stuff?" Brad asked, pointing at the radios.

Sean reached down and picked up a handset. He powered up a radio and hit a scan button. "Looks like a basic setup, shouldn't be too difficult to use," he said.

The radio stopped its scan and they heard static and a broken noise. It was hard to tell if they were hearing just static or a garbled voice. Sean pressed the scan again, but it never stopped and looped back through to the garbled frequency.

"Mayday, mayday, mayday, any station," Sean said into the handset. When he released the handset they heard the same garbled static.

"Sounds like there's nothing out there, and whatever is on this station is probably high powered and blocking the freq. Let's set up a radio watch; maybe we'll get lucky," Sean said.

Brad was looking through the drawers of the workspace and found a large, clothbound book. He opened it and looked inside. "Hey check this out. It's a logbook," he said as he flipped through the pages.

Sean and Brooks turned and leaned over the book. All of the entries were handwritten in dark ink. Brad turned through the entries page by page until, more than halfway through, the text changed. Instead of generic entries about dial readings and counters, there were more detailed journal entries.

"Look at the writing. Instead of operator entries, the platform manager has taken over the log," Brad said.

Sean looked at the entry on the page and pointed at the number. "That was over thirty days ago; right about the time of the outbreak," he said.

Moving his finger down the page, Brad found the first detailed entry and began reading.

Log Date 214:

First Officer J.C. Sharif Assumes the Log.

08:00 - The resupply ferry did not arrive. Men are angry and ready to return home. The satellite television is reporting news of riots and violence on the mainland. PAK-PETROL said they will give us detailed information later and reschedule the ferry.

17:00 - We were contacted by PAK-PETROL Corporate. Our resupply ferry has been delayed. Problem is at the mainline Karachi ferry station, described as mechanical in nature. They will notify us when the ferry is back online. The men doubt this as family members have relayed news to us of a pandemic hitting the mainland, people are getting sick. We think Corporate is keeping us in the dark so that we will keep working and not abandon the platform.

Log Date 215:

14:00 - Satellite TV is showing worldwide martial law in effect. People are rioting and attacking anyone. Citizens are warned to stay indoors, stay away from hospitals and avoid city streets. Corporate denies the reports and says news of violence is exaggerated; Corporate promised the ferry will be coming soon.

Log Date 216:

06:00 - We picked up radio traffic from the cargo ship 'Chang' this morning. Chang warned us to turn away any unknown vessels. They had spotted a ship dead in the water and boarded it. The crew of the disabled vessel attacked their boarding party. They sought help from the Coast Guard but were turned away and warned not to approach the coastal waters.

10:00 - We have halted production as our storage containers are now full.

12:00 - *One of the engineers was able to contact his family with the satellite phone. Family said that hospitals are shut down. The cities are overrun with rioters. The Pakistani Army has been mobilized and is threatening nuclear retaliation against India for inciting violence against the people. This all makes no sense.*

Log Date 217:

08:00 - We have depleted fresh rations, we have thirty plus days of canned goods, desalinization is working normally, the satellite TV is broadcasting on a loop, we have not been able to reach anyone on the satellite phone. The men are panicking.

14:00 - Message from Corporate received via UHF, the ferry station has been closed. We have been told to hold out and await transport. The men are restless and threatening desertion.

Log Date 218:

05:00 - Ten men deserted the platform today and fled in the small boat. A note found in the boathouse said they were returning to their families.

08:00 - Fishing vessel approached the sea deck. They requested permission to dock. The security team met and escorted them onto the first deck. Our doctor inspected the crew; they were hungry and dehydrated but no visible signs of illness. The Captain of the fishing boat said that the mainland ports are all closed. He was forced to seek refuge in blue water. Coast Guard ships are firing on anything that approaches the shore. We have allowed them refuge; we may need their vessel if the ferry does not arrive.

14:00 - We were approached by a small craft from the Pakistani Navy. The five man crew were injured and seeking medical attention. We brought them to the infirmary for treatment by the doctor. They had visible wounds, cuts and scrapes and were suffering from high fever. During the night the crew became agitated and attacked and killed the doctor and our medic. We locked them in the infirmary. They are contained but cannot be reasoned with.

Log Date 219:

10:00 - We have been boarded by Pakistani Navy war ship. They have taken control of the platform. When informed about their crew members in the infirmary, a team was dispatched to take care of them. They executed the sick crew members and disposed of the bodies over the rail. Pakistani Navy has commandeered the bottom two decks. All of our team members have been ordered to occupy the top deck only.

Log Date 220:

12:00 - PAK-PETROL Ferry arrived today with crew members from other platforms. Instead of taking us home they are seeking refuge on the platform. A large United States Navy war ship has attached to the platform. U.S. Military helicopter dropped off American Military to platform. We have been ordered to surrender control of operations to the U.S. Military. We have nowhere to go.

15:00 - U.S. Military has ordered all non-essential team members to report to lower decks for evacuation processing. Only Engineers and those required to maintain platform life support will be allowed above the second deck. Log closed. J.C. Sharif.

Brad finished reading the handwritten pages and took a step away from the desk. He turned to look out of the observation window that overlooked the platform. The ocean had a calming effect. The hot sun was burning down on the deck outside, and he could see the men working, cleaning the deck, and patrolling. Brad looked back down at the desk and Sean closed the journal.

"What the hell are we going to do, Chief?" Brad asked.

"I'm not sure, Brad. Let's get one of the Marines to sit on this radio. We need to get a planning session together with the officers. This place might start feeling cozy after a couple of days, but we can't stay here. Our focus has to be on leaving."

Brooks stood up from the log book and clipped his MP5 back onto his body armor. "Sounds good, Chief. I'll get one of the guys trained on these radios and we can all meet up on the helipad in a couple hours. I say the sooner we get out of here the better."

15.

Brad slowly walked around the platform's rail, following the entire perimeter of the first deck while trying to clear his head. The platform's systems were all back online; he could hear the hum of the pumps and the rattle of machinery in the power house. Brad turned a corner near the storage deck and found Corporal Swanson directing a couple of the men in breaking down pallets of supplies. She smiled when she saw him and turned to walk in his direction.

"Hi Brad," she called out.

"Hello Chelsea, how is everything coming along? Any problems?"

"Everything is going great now that we have all of the lights back on and the boilers are cranking out hot water. I was breaking down some of this gear. I thought with the power on we could cook a nice meal tonight."

"Sounds great Chelsea, good to hear," Brad said softly.

"Really? Then why do you look so down?"

"It's just been a long few weeks. I thought I had a goal I was working toward, but now I just want to sit down and rest. You ever get that feeling?"

"Every day, Brad, but once you allow yourself to quit, it will be hard as hell to keep going. We have to just keep pushing, you know. Doesn't matter what for, just keep pushing. Don't quit, okay?"

"Okay Chelsea," Brad said, cracking a smile.

"So where are you headed anyhow? Would you mind some company?" she asked him.

"I'm going up to the helipad to meet with Chief and the pilots. We're trying to figure out how to get off this thing. You're welcome to come along."

Brad waited for Chelsea to brief the Marines before she joined him on his path to the helipad. They climbed the stairs to the top, where they found the officers had attached long fuel lines to the Blackhawk and were gassing it up. Sean and Brooks were standing over the apron of the pad looking down at the sea, so Brad and Chelsea moved in to join them.

They could see all the way to the water. A fishing boat still drifted quiet and lonely at the length of a long line. The small military boat was in bad shape, now listing to one side. The large fast attack craft was still there, attached to the deck by a number of mooring lines. Sean and Brooks were in a deep discussion over the military vessel's capabilities.

"Hey Brad, I see you brought a friend," Sean said, acknowledging the presence of Swanson.

"Yeah Chief, I figure she has just as much at stake in this as any of us."

"Good call. Welcome to the head shed, Swanson," Sean said smiling.

"Thanks Chief, so what's the plan?" Chelsea answered.

"Well, that's what we are trying to decipher. Captain Bradley, are you two about finished?" Sean called out across the platform.

Captain Bradley walked from around the nose of the aircraft, wiping his hands with an oil-stained rag. Mr. Douglas was close behind him. Brad watched as Bill turned a number of fuel cutoff valves and disconnected the fuel lines from the aircraft.

"All settled here, Chief. We have her completely topped off. With the external tanks full, we have a range of nearly a thousand miles. All we need is a destination," Captain Bradley said as he walked to the railing and leaned against it. Mr. Douglas came in close and took a seat on the deck, opening a bottle of water.

"That's the problem, we have no comms with anyone and nobody is answering the phone, so where in the hell do we go?" Sean said.

"Socotra," Bill called out.

"What? What the hell is a Socotra?" Brooks asked as they all turned to look at Bill, who was now walking in their direction, having finished stowing the fuel lines.

"Socotra. It's an island about a thousand miles from here, off the horn of Africa. I did some exploratory drilling near there with the company in the late nineties," Bill said, unrolling a map.

He laid the large map out flat on the deck and pointed to the island. "I heard our sailors talking about it. The island is just off the coast of Yemen. Not many folks live there and they said it was infection-free. Well it *was* anyway."

"What exactly did the sailors say ,Bill?" Sean asked.

"I don't know a lot. They were pretty quiet about it, but rumor had it that the U.S. military had occupied the island and they were staging things there. The island has a small airport. We even heard a carrier strike group was plugged into the island."

Brooks put his hand on the map and drew a line with his finger from the platform to the island. "A thousand miles, that's a hell of a haul," Brooks said, looking at the map. "I don't know if we could take that patrol boat across the open water, but I would be more comfortable hugging the coast."

"How old is this information?" Sean asked.

Bill scratched the side of his head and squinted. "Well, I figure it's been at least three weeks since I heard it. You kind of lose track of time out here."

Mr. Douglas stared at the map. "That's going to stretch the limits of the chopper. I don't think we can make it on one hop without getting wet."

Swanson leaned over the map and pointed at a small island off the coast of Oman. There was a small airport symbol at its northernmost point. "What's this, sir? Could you fly here?" she asked.

Captain Bradley looked at the island. "Masirah Air Base, yeah, that's about five hundred miles. We could make that, but is it safe? It's not like we can turn around and go home if it's not."

Brooks looked at the chart and then went to look over the rail at the attack craft. "I would feel a lot better about taking that boat five hundred miles than a thousand. But we don't know shit about that place; what if we get there and it's overrun?" he asked.

Sean took the map and drew a circle around the island. "It looks isolated enough, and it's within our range. I say we go for it. We may even find a suitable fixed wing there to take us home. But how do we travel: sea, air, or both?"

Brad sat listening to the conversation, taking it all in. He wasn't a fan of the ocean, but he had never been very comfortable with flying, either. That's why he'd joined the Army instead of the Navy or the Air Force. Today though, his options were very limited.

He chimed in, "Absolutely by air … I mean, if the pilots are comfortable with the distance. We don't know the condition of the boat yet. But the map shows a port, also, so let's ready the aircraft while we secure that ship and see if it's seaworthy."

Captain Bradley examined the map again, using his finger to estimate the distance. "Shouldn't be a problem finding it, but I'm somewhat worried about the aircraft. It's really overdue for some heavy maintenance. We picked it up off an abandoned airfield weeks ago and, other than fuel and washing the windows, we haven't done much to it."

"It's your call, sir," Sean said.

Bradley smiled and, leaning back against the rail with his hands in his pockets, said, "I'm willing to give it a shot then."

Sean took the map and rolled it up before handing it back to Bill. "Okay, we have a short term plan then. Captain Bradley, prep your aircraft for the trip to Masirah. You will take Bill as your crew chief, and one of the Marines as a gunner. I have the rest. Tomorrow … mid-day … we'll assault the ship and take it back."

The helipad cleared out quickly after the meeting. Bill had asked Chelsea to give him a hand refueling the generators, and Brad once again found himself alone. He moved down the stairs and wound his way along the walkway till he reached the center deck facing the disabled lift. The space was clear now; there was no evidence of the small skirmish from earlier in the day when they had lost one of their own.

Wilson and Nelson were on watch. He greeted them and moved closer to the exposed mouth of the lift, looking into the dark space while keeping his distance.

There was a mashed bit of flesh and blood at the lip of the deck below the opening. "What happened here?" Brad asked.

Wilson stepped forward, trying to conceal a grin. "Ahh ... well ... one of them things kept sticking its hand out every time we got too close to the opening. I guess we kind of smashed its fingers with the sledge. Yeah ... it ain't been doing that anymore."

Brad shook his head at them. "Just don't do anything stupid, okay? Have you noticed any changes out of them?"

Nelson stepped a bit closer to the lip and shone his flashlight into the space. "No, Sergeant, they just stand there ... staring at us."

Brad moved closer and squatted to the deck. He peered into the gap and could see the pale face of a man looking back at him. Its eyes were focused and intense. Brad could almost feel the hatred of the thing. It was like looking into the eyes of a vicious dog and knowing there would be no reasoning, no calming it down. Brad made eye contact with the primal and it suddenly bared its teeth and lunged forward.

Brad flinched heavily, losing his balance and falling over on his backside. The two Marines laughed. Wilson extended a hand to Brad and pulled him back to his feet. "Don't be ashamed, Sergeant, that son of a bitch got me a couple times too," he said. "I wish we could just shoot them all; I hate looking at these damn things."

"Sergeant, do you really think them things operated the lift?" Nelson asked.

Brad looked back at him. "No, I don't. You put a monkey in an elevator long enough and it will eventually start pushing buttons. I think they just got lucky. Either way, don't worry about that, just keep your head in the game."

"Yes Sergeant," Nelson replied.

"Looks like you fellas have everything under control out here; I'm going to head back. I'll send someone to relieve you when chow is ready. Stay safe," Brad said.

16.

The men gathered in the platform's main galley. With the life support systems powered up, the kitchen was operational. Tony and Mr. Douglas had raided the pantries and stores of supplies on the deck and managed to put together a hell of a pot of chili. Tony had offered up another bottle of his finest Kentucky bourbon, but this time Chief had declined.

There was a lot of work to be done before they assaulted the attack boat, and he wanted everyone to be sharp. The men feasted on the hot chow until their bellies were full. Casual conversations filled the deck, the war stories and joking that had always accompanied meals back in the world. After dinner, the Marines went about their business of cleaning and maintaining their equipment while the pilots looked over charts, plotting their possible venture to the Masirah airbase.

Those that weren't working were relaxing in the lounge or preparing for the night's watch out on the decks. They had set up guard rotations with three-man teams around the clock: two patrolling the deck and one on the radio. There were only eleven of them now, with the loss of Ben. The rotations were four-hour shifts, with Brad and Brooks filling the holes and taking the extra watches at the radio.

As the sun went down, the men heard the scurrying of movement on the decks below. The primals were reminding them that they were still there, that they owned the lower decks and the darkness. As the patrols walked the deck grating, they could hear the primals moan and scream below them. The darker and cooler the night got, the bolder the primals became. It was a nerve-racking duty, but a price they had to pay to keep the deck secure.

Sean and Brooks met in one of the offices and planned out the assault on the vessel. This was their expertise, and Brad trusted them to do the right thing. Brad had grown up on the Great Lakes and had some experience onboard small boats, but nothing like this. His most ambitious voyages were short day trips on a thirty-footer, doing some fishing on Lake Superior. Brad left the SEALs alone and made his way to the control tower to start his shift on the radios.

Brad sat at the radio slowly turning the dials, switching between UHF and VHF. After he had gone the entire length of the dial with no response, he set the console to 'scan'. Brooks had managed to get one of the small computers working and found that it had a rudimentary radar application installed. Brad could see the large globe and dish spinning just outside the window, letting him know that the radar hardware was running.

Brad cycled through the filters while following the notes Brooks had scribbled on a sheet of paper. He could barely make out the coast as a jagged blurred line nearly sixty miles to their north. The radar was set to max scan and he occasionally saw static or surface noise on the screen, but nothing that would obviously identify itself as a ship. Brad cycled from surface to air to weather, noting nothing of interest or anything worth logging.

He picked up the log book. They had opened it back up and had begun using it again. He scanned the entries of the earlier watches: 'Nothing to report' and 'all conditions normal'. Just as he was beginning to think they were alone, the radio scanner locked on a station. It was garbled and broken, but appeared to be in English. Brad turned up the volume and manually tweaked the tuning knob. He listened intently and struggled to transcribe the broken, static-filled message.

"Ma...ay, ...ayday, ...ay. This is the ...rench vessel ...dupar calling all ...ons.
May... ...ay, ...day, ... Captain ... of ves... dupar... ead... water... ...irty males ...board.
Locat... is North ...45 ...st 67... ...12."

"Last calling station, say again," Brad yelled into the microphone.

Silence.

"Last calling station, say again," he tried once more.

The radio had again gone silent. Brad logged the communication and looked at the notes. It was impossible to determine anything from the broken call for help, but he would hand the notes to Sean when he left his shift. Brad checked the radar scope again for any vessel and finally gave up in frustration.

Private Craig came to relieve him just after midnight. Brad quickly refreshed the private on the use of the console. He told him about the broken radio contact and left word for him to send a runner if he heard anything else from the ship. Then Brad waited for the rest of his patrol to pass by the building so he could join them on his way back to the living quarters. They had set up a strict policy of 'no one goes outside alone after dark'.

As they walked the grates, Brad could hear the primals following below; the sounds of footsteps and the labored panting were like being pursued by a pack of wolves. Brad stopped, asking the two Marines to hold up. He pulled a flashlight from his belt and shined it between the gaps in the grating. What he saw spooked him and he quickly turned out the light. He looked to the left and could tell that the Marines had seen it too.

"Holy shit, Sergeant, there are hundreds of them down there," Private Nelson muttered with fear in his voice.

"Well it's nothing we didn't know, right? We secured the lift, ladders, and the stairs; they can't get up here," Brad tried to reassure the private.

"I'll be glad when we leave this damn place," Nelson whispered.

"Me too Private … me too."

As Brad arrived back at the third floor, he found Sean sitting in the lounge cleaning his equipment. Brad handed him the note and told him about the radio contact. Sean took the note and read it as Brad explained the contact and how the radar scope had been clear.

"Shit, wish there was something we could do for them. That signal could have bounced for hundreds ... even thousands of miles. No telling how far away they are," Sean said, reading the message.

"Yeah I know. It just sucks, man. Be nice to get some good news for a change. I put Craig on the frequency and told him to wake me if it comes back," Brad said.

"That's all you can do, Brad, now get some sleep. I'm going to need you to be sharp tomorrow," Sean said, turning back to his equipment.

Some of the other men were also still up in the lounge, preparing for their watch, not able to sleep, or just avoiding sleep altogether. Sleeping was not a thing people enjoyed on the platform. Often it ended being awakened by nightmares, sometimes by the screams of your buddy in the cell next door as he relived the events of the past month. They all worked until they were exhausted, until avoiding sleep wasn't an option, but they rarely got more than four hours before they found themselves back in the lounge.

Brad used his free time and took advantage of the running water to shower and do laundry. It was a recent luxury to have a functioning laundry room and latrine. With the stores of food and the life support systems, Brad wondered if he might be tempted to stay here if they *could* somehow remove the primals. At least until the food and fuel ran out.

His thoughts drifted back to the men in the compound and the promise he had made to them. Brad lay back in his bunk, holding one of PFC Ryan's dog tags in his hand, knowing the other was buried on the man back in the Afghan sand. It was a stern reminder that it wasn't his mission to find a safe refuge. It was his job to seek rescue for his men. That he was, and would always be, on the clock until he got them all home.

Brad placed the dog tag on his night stand, then checked his good luck charm: the unfired S&W pistol. He pulled back the slide to make sure a round was chambered, then placed it within arm's reach. Brad reached up behind him and cut the light, drifting to sleep with the sounds of the humming generators calming his nerves.

17.

It was go time. Tony was in the cab of the crane. A large steel cable had been looped over the ball and hook that extended from the end of the crane's arm. Brooks had attached another two hundred and fifty feet of heavy rappelling line to the end of the hook. The SEALs sat on the rail with the ball and hook just over their heads. On command, Tony would swing them out over the open water and lower them to the boat below.

Sean had synced his wireless headset to the radio in the cab. He gave Tony the word to move them. Brad watched as the crane swung out away from the platform, the SEALs dangling beneath it. Sean and Brooks were dressed in bright green dive suits and swim fins that had been salvaged from a locker on the platform. The men had tried to camouflage or at least darken the colors with grease, but the attempt only made them look worse.

The crane swung out and abruptly jerked to a stop, swinging the men out and away uncontrollably. Sean reached out at the length of his arm and grabbed the steel cable, stabilizing them. He turned back and shot Tony a cold stare. Tony put his hands up apologetically and then gave Sean a thumbs up. Brooks nodded back and unclipped his D-ring, then began a slow descent to the attack craft below.

Brad changed positions farther down the railing so he could see the boat hundreds of feet below. He held his rifle at the ready but was not confident he would be much good if he needed to fire at such a steep angle. Brad watched as Brooks descended, then slowed and hung barely twenty feet above the surface of the water. Sean slid down the length of the rope, stopped just above Brooks, and placed himself into an over watch position with his suppressed MP5 at the ready.

Once Sean was in a comfortable position, Brooks continued his decent and cut into the water. Brad watched as Brooks disconnected himself from the line and quietly swam to the side of the attack boat before he slipped under the water. After several seconds, Brad watched him surface near the dock with his dive knife in hand.

Slowly and quietly he cut the rope holding the smaller boat to the dock, allowing the small damaged military craft to drift free and away from the platform. He then swam closer to the attack boat and, finding the mooring lines too big to cut, pulled himself out of the water and onto the dock. Brad felt his heart race as he tried to get an angle to cover his friend.

Brad watched the larger ship also begin to slowly drift free and away from the platform. On closer inspection, he could just make out Brooks' head barely sticking above the surface of the water; he was holding one of the heavy lines and signaling for Tony to lower the hook and cable. The crane swung and came back to life.

Next, Sean was slowly lowered into the water. He swam the lead line to Brooks and together they pulled it until the end of the steel cable was in their hands. Working together, they attached the cable to one of the heavy mooring lines. Tony took the slack out of the line and carefully guided the boat out away from the dock and close to one of the four large pylons that anchored the rig to the sea bed.

Brooks swam close to the pylon and tied the attack craft off to a series of pinion hooks embedded in the base of the structure just above the water line. Once the boat was secured to the pylon, Sean reached up and released the cable from the vessel and allowed it to swing free. Tony raised the cable up and away from the boat below while Brooks and Sean pulled themselves onto the dive deck at the rear of the vessel and ducked down, hiding.

Tony quickly raised the hook back to the third deck and swung it in towards the rail. Bill immediately unhooked the steel cable from the ball and hook, then hurriedly attached a large basket to the end of the ball and motioned to Brad that it was ready. The basket was nothing more than a steel cage the size of a phone booth. Bill opened a gate on the basket and ushered them in. Brad shook his head but willed himself forward and stepped into the basket with Wilson and Craig, weapons at the ready.

They held on tight as Tony raised them up and swung them out over the water. The crane again stopped quickly, swinging them out hard. They swung back and forth several times before slowing, and Tony began lowering them down toward the vessel. Brad looked out over the edge of the basket as it passed the second deck. It was far worse than he had imagined.

A series of elevated cat walks surrounded by heavy pipes and drilling equipment covered the second deck. The walkways were littered with the dead. The sun was high in the sky, leaving the deep internal area of the deck shaded and in the dark. Brad squinted in the contrasting lights, trying to search for movement. There was little he could see but he knew they were there, hiding in a maze of walkways.

The basket continued its descent until it was just above the vessel. As they got closer, Brad was finally able to take in the size of the attack boat. It was over a hundred feet long and painted in a grey camouflage pattern. He could see a turret on the bow – possibly a 30mm, maybe 40mm gun; it reminded him of the Bushmaster he had seen on the Bradley fighting vehicles. There were at least two .50 caliber machine guns on the rear platform.

The bow was completely covered with metal deck plating. Brad could see a walkway that horseshoed around the large bridge structure and continued beyond onto the rear deck. The bridge held large, tinted windows, but Brad could barely see inside over the reflective glass. The interior looked empty, but the side doors leading to the walkways were open, swinging along with the swells of the sea. A large array of antennas and radar dishes sat motionless along the top of the bridge structure.

The rear deck of the ship was vacant except for a large rigid hull inflatable strapped to a rack. Brad couldn't see evidence of a battle or even a struggle on the decks; if there had been one, then the storms of the last week must have washed it away. Looking farther back, Brad could just barely make out the lime green silhouettes of the SEALs crouched low on the dive deck.

Tony swung them to the left and right, trying to drop them precisely onto a cleared space over the covered bow of the attack boat. They touched the surface of the ship with a metallic crunch; the vessel briefly bobbed away from them, then rose and made a screech as the basket dragged. Tony let out more line, taking the weight of the basket off the crane and putting it onto the bow.

Craig quickly jumped from the basket and helped to steady it as Wilson and Brad followed him onto the bow of the ship. Once they were clear, Tony began raising it away from the boat. They immediately checked their surroundings, making sure they were alone. Spotting cover, Brad and the Marines walked hunched over and hid behind the bow-mounted gun turret.

The noise of their landing did not go unnoticed. They heard the screaming moans start from the second deck. Brad looked up just in time to see a primal run at them and leap into the water. He watched the primal fly out and away from the platform before plunging over a hundred feet to the water's surface. The primal hit the water with a sickening crack.

Brad then watched the creature begin to slip below the surface before it shuddered awake and tried to swim towards them. Craig raised his rifle and shot it twice in the head, ending the primal's struggle. Before they could look away they heard three more screaming as they also flew through the air and smacked the water. Craig and Wilson took aimed shots at these creatures as well as they moved and struggled to stay afloat. As fast as they could shoot them, more dropped into the sea, jumping from the high platform.

Screaming and a rush of feet came from behind them. Brad turned to watch a mad rush of primals fill the bridge windows. They ran and crashed at the glass but failed to break through it. The primals left the bridge, found the walkway, and attempted to make their way out onto the bow to get at Brad and the Marines. Sean and Brooks broke cover from the dive deck and cut them down with their MP5s as they crossed their paths.

Brad pulled the Marines back into cover to prevent them from being hit by the SEALs' crossfire. He heard more splashing and the sound of primals impacting the water. Brad grabbed Craig's shoulder and faced him in the direction of the splashes. He ordered the Marines to concentrate their fire on the primals leaping from the deck while he covered the walkways. Simultaneously he heard more gunfire and rounds hit the water.

Looking up, he could see that Swanson and the others had joined the fight. They were taking long shots from the top deck, firing at the struggling creatures in the water. Brad heard the SEALs' fire wither and turned to see the last of the primals crumple at the edge of the walkway. Looking back at the platform, he saw that the primals' strategy had changed.

The primals were running down the ladder wells to the bottom deck where they swarmed the docks, howling and screaming at the water's edge. Occasionally one would step forward and leap into the sea. Brad and the Marines watched the primals struggle in the water. Apparently they were not good swimmers, as most of them sank beneath the surface after only going ten to fifteen feet.

The attack boat was safety tied off to the pylon at least forty feet from the dock, so Brad ordered his men to cease fire. The primals were no longer a threat, and he didn't want to expend hundreds of rounds of ammunition on them. The Marines held their kneeling position with their weapons up and closely watched the primals as they howled. There were over a hundred of them massed along the edge of the dock. Looking up, there must have been close to a hundred more looking down from the second level.

Sean and Brooks moved forward from the dive deck, slowly clearing everything as they moved towards the bow. Sticking to the outside of the boat, Brooks shut and dogged the hatches as he passed them. Finally, they crept up alongside of Brad and the Marines and stood with them. Brooks unzipped the front of his wetsuit and leaned against the turret, looking at the screaming primals on the dock.

"Look at all of them! I'm glad we didn't decide to push down to the lower decks," Brooks said.

"No shit. I don't think we would have gotten through them. We would have been overrun for sure," Brad answered.

"Nahh, we would have made it, come on, Brad. This was just smarter," Sean joked.

"What are we going to do with all of them?" Wilson gasped, his voice cracking.

"For now, we aren't going to do anything with them; just keep an eye on them, okay?" Sean said before turning his back and speaking to Tony over his headset.

Moments later the crane started dropping the basket again with Swanson and Nelson on board. As it got closer, Brooks grabbed it and directed it toward a flat spot on the deck. Nelson jumped out first with a large kit bag in each hand. Once Brooks made sure they were clear and the gear was on the bow, he flashed a thumbs up skyward. Tony again pulled the basket up and away from the boat.

Quickly Sean and Brooks took the bags from Nelson and opened them. They peeled the wetsuits off and changed back into their combat uniforms and armor. They removed the silencers from their MP5s and attached flashlights and lasers to them. It only took a few minutes and the SEALs were back on their feet and ready for the second leg of this mission.

"Corporal, I need you and Nelson to watch the decks. Keep an eye on their movement. Call out to us if you see any changes. Try not to fire on them, but don't be afraid to shoot if you have to. I'm just worried about stray rounds starting a fire if you shoot towards the platform," Sean said.

"Got it, Chief," Swanson said as she and Nelson moved closer to the bow and took up kneeling positions where they could observe the crowds on the docks.

"Okay Brad, it's show time. Brooks and I will assault from the engine room hatch and through the hull. I want you three to pop that door and secure the bridge. Like before, watch what you are shooting at. We actually want to be able to drive this boat when we're done, so don't go wild shooting shit up. Any questions?" Sean said.

"Understood. My team is going to assault and secure the bridge. We're on it, Chief," Brad answered.

"Good, give us a minute to set up on the back deck and go on my movement," Sean said as he slapped Brooks on the back.

Brad watched the SEALs move back down the platform toward the back deck, then turned and looked Craig and Wilson in the eye. "Wilson, you're my point man. Craig, back him up. I'll direct our movements from just behind you. Move slow Wilson, this isn't a race. Just like in training, guys," Brad whispered to them as they moved toward the door.

"Just like training, my ass," Wilson said. "I'm an equipment mechanic, not a door kicker."

"Well then, I guess now is a good time for some on-the-job training," Brad said.

They moved forward and stacked up on the port side door leading to the bridge. Brad looked back at Swanson and Nelson, who were intently watching the crazed mobs on the docks. Feeling his stare, Swanson looked back at him and gave him a thumbs up. Brad returned the gesture and took up the six-position on the stack at the door.

Wilson had his rifle at the ready and waited for the go signal. Craig was just behind Wilson, his left hand on Wilson's back and his rifle in his shoulder. Brad was staggered just slightly, leaning out with his hand on the door handle ready to launch it in. "I know what Chief said, but if you have to fire, take the shots. I'd rather have damaged equipment than lose one of you guys," Brad whispered.

Before the Marines could respond, they heard the clang of the engine room hatch and then the bang as it was thrown open against the deck. "Go!" Brad said as he pulled down on the handle and shoved the door in.

"Next man in, right!" Wilson yelled as he cleared the doorway.

"Coming in, right," Craig called just behind him as he cut through the narrow doorway and took a position aiming down the right side of the bridge.

Brad pulled in just behind them, aiming down the center. The bridge was about fifteen feet wide and had two large chairs positioned near the steering controls. Brad could see navigation equipment scattered around the large consoles on the far wall. Two dead crew members lay on the floor in solid blue jump suits. A small sub machine gun lay on the deck with an empty magazine lying near it.

Even with the tinted windows, the sun easily lit the space. Brad gestured for them to move forward online. He could hear the SEALs moving through the bowels of the ship; an occasion muffled gunshot or a shout of instruction reverberated up through the hull. There were two ladders leaving the bridge, one leading aft and the other in and under the bow.

Both ladder ways had their hatches open. Brad signaled for Craig to dog the aft hatch so they could focus their attention towards the bow. Craig pushed the hatch but failed to close it. On closer inspection, he saw part of a man's leg blocking the bottom quarter of the door. Brad moved around the door to look down the ladder well and into the darkened interior of the ship.

Brad couldn't see anything below, but he could hear the echoes of the SEALs' movements. He used his boot to kick the man's leg clear of the hatch, then helped Craig push it shut and secure its latches. Just as they secured the final latch, they heard the rapid firing of Wilson's rifle. Brad turned just in time to see two crazies already directly in front of Wilson, coming up the ladder and through the hatch.

Wilson was firing point blank into a uniformed primal's chest, but the momentum of a second primal pushed it forward and onto the Marine. Wilson tripped and fell onto his back; flailing, he dropped his rifle to the side. Brad lowered his weapon and fired at the second primal that was now lying across Wilson's hips. At the same time, Craig smacked the head of the uniformed creature with the butt stock of his rifle.

Brad leapt forward and kicked the second primal hard enough to knock him clear off of Wilson and back down the stairs. Craig had regained control of his rifle and fired three rounds into the head of the other primal. He then grabbed Wilson and dragged him clear of the bow hatch as Brad slammed it shut and locked its latches.

Wilson was still on the ground flailing about. Brad grabbed him and tried to calm him as he inspected his body for wounds. He stopped cold when he saw a large gash going from Wilson's right hip and down the side of his leg. Brad ripped the clothing away to get a better look at the wound. It didn't look good. Brad could see deep into the muscle; blood was oozing out and filling the cut.

Brad put pressure on the area and ordered Craig to give him a tourniquet. Brad ripped the rest of the clothing away and tried to apply the tourniquet but the location of the wound made it impossible. He grabbed a bundle of pressure dressings off of the Marine's body armor and started packing them around the long gash. Wilson was still flailing on the deck and screaming.

"They fucking got me, oh shit they got me, Sergeant they got me," Wilson screamed.

"No, it's okay Wilson. Maybe you cut it on the hatch or when you fell. It's okay," Brad said back, trying to calm the Marine.

"No, he fucking got me, I felt it. I felt its hands rip at me. He got me."

"Calm down, Marine, and let us work. Craig, get down here and put pressure on this wound," Brad ordered.

Craig switched positions and put both hands on the open cut. Brad used his knife to cut more material from the Marine's other pant leg. He looked back up at Wilson's face just in time to see…

"NO!"

Wilson had drawn his side arm and had the barrel in his mouth; Brad lunged forward to grab it just as Wilson pulled the trigger.

Brad punched the deck before dropping on his back side and sitting flat on the floor. Craig released his grip on Wilson's leg and just stared at him in shock. The bridge was suddenly quiet, the smell of Wilson's blood and the gunpowder filling the air. Brad got to his feet and began to walk outside just as someone banged on the aft hatch. "It's us, open the hatch," he heard Brooks yell.

Brad stopped and walked to the aft hatch and undogged the latches to allow the hatch to open. Without saying a word, Brad turned and walked out of the bridge and back onto the deck of the ship. Sean followed Brad through the doorway and looked at him.

"Sergeant! Get back on the bridge and cover your man. Brooks and I will clear the bow," Sean ordered.

Brad looked at Sean with a scowl, then slowly readied his weapon and followed him back onto the bridge. Brad looked down at the still body of Wilson. Craig and Brooks were busy moving the primals away from the bow hatch, preparing to open the door. Once the way was clear, Brooks leaned against the wall and signaled for Craig to unlock it.

The door swung out and the two SEALs dropped down the ladder. Moments later he heard them give the 'all clear'. Brad reached down and grabbed Wilson by the shoulders. He asked Craig to help carry him out onto the deck. Craig nodded and let his rifle hang from the sling as he grabbed Wilson by the ankles and followed Brad through the hatch.

They sat Wilson's body just outside the door on the deck. Brad removed his dog tags and put them in his pocket.

"This isn't your fault, Sergeant," Craig said.

"I shouldn't have taken my eyes off of that hatch. Wilson was my responsibility," Brad said quietly.

"That's bullshit! Wilson was supposed to be watching the bow hatch; he got caught up on us trying to close the other door. He took his eyes off of his area; it was a mistake and it got him killed. It's not your fault," Craig argued.

"Well thank you for saying so, but it doesn't matter now; he's dead and we won't get him back."

Brad walked forward toward the bow of the ship. When he got to the front, he looked Swanson in the eyes, reached out his hand, and gave her the dog tags. She gasped when she read the name. "Where is he?" she asked, just above a whisper.

"Over there." Brad said, pointing down the walkway toward the bridge. "I'm sorry."

Swanson climbed to her feet and walked in the direction of the bridge.

18.

There was no time for mourning. Sean quickly put them all to work preparing the boat for departure. They dumped overboard nearly everything on the craft that wasn't bolted down. Working through the night, they cleaned every crevice with bleach to remove any contamination that might lurk on a sharp corner. While they decontaminated, Bill and Tony rigged pallets of supplies that they lowered down to the ship.

Brooks explained that the fast attack boat was normally operated by a crew of twenty, but they would have to make do with six. Tony had turned out to be an expert with the boat's large diesel engines; he was able to get the ship's power on and the motors purred to life. The diesel engines allowed them to fully power up the systems on the bridge. Brooks gave the craft a walk down and determined it to be in good working order.

The sleeping compartment was filled with goods. They stacked cases of MREs in the bunks, and cases of fresh water anyplace they could fit them. One advantage to running on a skeleton crew was that it allowed for more storage space. Brooks estimated they should have enough food for forty-five days on board; fuel would be the problem.

The boat had a range of approximately eight hundred miles on full tanks. They had lowered two pallets of fuel drums and strapped those to the rear deck. They debated bringing on more fuel drums, but Brooks and Sean feared overloading the vessel. They had to be cautious taking the small boat into blue water, so they wanted it as stable as possible.

Crews had been selected and assigned responsibilities. Craig would travel in the Blackhawk with Bill. Tony and Swanson were assigned to the boat's engine room. Nelson had an electrical background, so Sean quickly appointed the private as the ship's electrician's mate. Brooks would control the vessel and promised to train Brad on the ship's weapons systems as they went. Sean, of course, would be the chief/captain of the boat.

They made plans to depart late the following afternoon. Brooks estimated it would take them close to eighteen hours to complete the five-hundred-mile trip to Masirah Island. If they left on time and sailed through the night, they should reach the island at the hottest part of the next day, when any primals that might occupy the island should hopefully be dormant.

The air crew made similar preparations. They would hold on station to give the boat a fourteen-hour head start. If everything went according to plan, they would take off early the morning after, and would arrive at the island near the same time as the surface team. Staggering their starts also allowed them to support each other. If the boat was halfway enroute and the air crew ran into problems, the attack boat would be the only hope for a water rescue.

By the end of the day, all of their gear had been pre-positioned on the boat or the helicopter, leaving only the bare essentials on the platform. Brooks and Tony had decided to stay the night on the vessel to make sure there would be no surprises on the next day's voyage. Sean was running around making final preparations and plans on how to idle the platform as they left.

Brad was back in the observation tower. He had been scanning the radio for the last couple of hours, searching for any signal, but so far had come up empty. The radar scope had also been blank. Brad stood and walked towards the windows, where he could see the men making their rounds as they patrolled the decks. After the death of Wilson, Brad had lost the urge to socialize. He had been focusing on work and the coming trip instead.

Brad sat back in the tower's chair and began slowly turning the tuning dial, still desperate to find a contact. He heard the door open and shut in the room below. He listened as the person below walked to the ladder and began climbing into the observation tower. Brad looked down into the face of Swanson. She grabbed the top rung of the ladder and pulled herself into the room.

"I noticed you skipped chow. I brought you some dinner, or at least this place's version of dinner," she said as she sat a covered plate on the desk in front of Brad.

Brad peeled the foil back from the plate. "Looks like maybe ... meatloaf? Well thank you Chelsea, I didn't have much of an appetite earlier."

He took the fork and took a large bite of the meat. Chelsea walked across the room and took a seat in an empty chair.

"You okay, Brad? You've been pretty quiet all evening," she said.

"I'm fine; I just needed to take a time out. It's been an exhausting couple of days."

Chelsea looked at the radios and reviewed the pages in the log book. "You pick up anything else?" she asked, changing the subject.

"Nope, scope has been clear and not a peep on the radio. It's damn quiet out here ... I'm so ready to leave this place," he said with a sigh.

"Me too, I can't wait to get going."

"So what are your plans? Where is home for you, Chelsea?"

"Home? I don't really know any more. I lived with my mom and sister in upstate New York before I joined the Corps, but last I heard New York is gone."

"I'm sure your family was evacuated; you'll find them," Brad said.

"Yeah, maybe ... What about you Brad, what will you do?"

"I hadn't thought much about it. I left a group of people back in Afghanistan. My first priority is to get them home. After that, I don't know, I'm guessing the Army will have plans for me. I have family in Michigan, but I don't know where things stand at home; I haven't been able to reach them since before the outbreak."

Their conversation was suddenly interrupted by the sound of gunfire. Brad jumped up to look through the observation window. He could see Craig standing with his rifle at his shoulder, firing rounds into the stairway on the storage deck. Captain Bradley was next to him with his M9 drawn and also firing. Bill had fallen in behind them holding a fire axe.

"What the hell is going on?" Brad said.

A siren began to blast.

"That's the automated alarm, something is wrong with the platform!" Chelsea exclaimed.

They heard the radio squawk. Brad grabbed the handset and looked at the channel. It was Brooks on the boat below.

"This is the tower, go ahead," Brad said into the handset.

"What the hell is going on up there? The primals are going nuts down here." Brooks said over the radio.

"I don't know, looks like they are attacking at the stairway. I need to get out there and help," Brad answered.

"What the fuck ... something is going on; there is oil pouring from the second deck. Tony said he thinks the purge valves must be open."

"Okay, I understand. I have to go; I have to find Bill," Brad said, putting down the handset and picking up his rifle. "Let's go, Chelsea, we need to get out there."

They slid down the ladder and back into the control room, quickly bursting outside and onto the deck. The sun had gone down, and the cool night air was filled with the sounds of gunfire and primal moans. Brad ran the walkway with Chelsea close behind him. When they arrived at the stairway to the second deck, they found Sean and Craig firing directly into it. Captain Bradley and Bill were just behind them, trying to force obstacles back into the barricade.

Brad ran forward and positioned himself next to Sean. He could see that the barricade below had collapsed onto the second deck. The pallets and crates they had stacked days earlier were harmlessly falling down the stairs, providing the primals a clear path to attack.

"What's going on here?" Brad yelled to Sean.

"They are going to breach, Brad, unless we plug this hole in a hurry. Somehow the sneaky fucks managed to take down the barrier without us knowing," Sean said.

Bill came up behind them on a small fork truck. He pressed another crate into the stairwell, temporarily closing the gap. Craig shifted positions and continued to shoot into the mass below them while Brad ran to the fork truck and waved his hands to get Bill's attention. Bill noticed him and cut the engine so he could hear.

"Bill, Tony said that the purge valves are open. Oil is pouring out onto the lower decks!" Brad yelled.

"No fucking way ... Chief! We have to get the hell out of here now!" Bill yelled. "If those valves are open, any spark could set this place off."

"Any spark?" Sean asked.

"Yeah *any* spark; like the ones coming out of your rifles," Bill replied.

"Craig! Cease fire!" Sean yelled just as more of the barricade collapsed. They could hear the primals at the bottom of the stack tearing away at the crates and pallets, trying to break through. "Captain Bradley, get your people airborne now. Brad, get Chelsea and Nelson to the boat, I am right behind you," Sean commanded.

"Who will operate the crane, Chief?" Chelsea asked.

"You don't need the crane, slide down the damn rope! Now hurry, we're running out of time," Sean barked.

Brad grabbed Chelsea by the wrist, dragging her behind him. "Where's Nelson?" he yelled.

"He had the late watch; he would have been off to bed early and may still be in the living quarters."

"Hurry! Follow me," Brad said just as they heard another crash and more of the barricade collapsed. They ran to the lounge and swung open the door. They found Nelson running down the hallway towards them.

"I heard the alarm, what's going on?" he asked.

"No time, follow us, we are abandoning the platform!" Brad yelled.

"Wait ... I have to go grab my kit," Nelson yelled back.

Chelsea reached forward, grabbed Nelson and shoved him towards the exit doors. "You have your rifle, Marine, that's all you need, let's go!"

Brad led the way, running down the walkway back toward the storage deck. He could hear the whining of the Blackhawk's engines as it powered up. The primals were screaming and there followed a flurry of activity on the deck below them. Brad rounded the corner and saw a cluster of primals just coming over the top of the barricade. Brad raised his rifle and fired into them.

He knocked the first two back but more filled the space. He ordered Chelsea and Nelson to run to the rail and get down to the boat. Chelsea hesitated, but turned and ran toward the railing. Brad moved farther away from the stairs in the direction of the railing, firing back as he went. More broke through and Brad took a knee and fired faster into the mass breaking through the stairway. For every one he hit, two more came over the crates searching for a handhold.

Brad looked to the railing just as Nelson clipped onto the cable and began the descent down. He watched as Chelsea hooked on to the cable and waited her turn to slide down. Another crash at the barricade turned his attention back to the primals. More of the crates had fallen and now there was a clear opening in the stairwell. The primals began filling the void two and three at a time. Brad fired quickly but he wasn't keeping up with the flood.

They broke through and charged at him. Brad fired several rounds, knocking many of them back. His bolt locked to the rear and he quickly ejected the magazine, keeping his eye on the sights to watch them bear down on his position. They were too close; he prepared to draw the S&W Sigma pistol. Suddenly Sean was standing over his shoulder; firing in full auto, sweeping the mass and pushing them back.

Brad re-holstered the Sigma and finished reloading his M4. He raised the rifle and started firing again as the mob rebounded. A full mass was now breaching the stairs. Sean ordered Brad to leave.

"Nah, I'm not feeling up to running today, Chief," Brad said as he leaned forward and continued to fire at the closing mass.

Sean's MP5 went dry and he pulled his sidearm, continuing to shoot into the closing wave. "It's been a pleasure to serve with you, Brad!" Sean yelled out as he killed two of them that had closed to within ten meters.

Brad saw them get closer and readied himself for the impact of the charging creatures. Leaning forward, he steeled his mind for the inevitable. He planned his demise in his own thoughts, everything slowing down. He knew he had ten, maybe twelve rounds left in the M4 and then he would have to draw his pistol. Fifteen shots – they would be on top of him by then. He would draw the karambit, that's how he would go, slashing and killing with his fists.

Brad fired the last round in the M4; he let the rifle hang from its sling and reached for his sidearm just as the deck in front of him exploded. Sparks of metal and fire filled his view as the primals were vaporized. He could feel the heat from the flames. Dazed, he realized that he'd been thrown backwards against the deck; looking into the sky, he saw the Blackhawk helicopter floating over his head. The helicopter's mini-gun was firing at full speed into the stairwell.

Brad felt suddenly peaceful; he had no strength to run, his legs were too heavy. Although Sean was slapping him, he couldn't feel the pain. His body was numb. He closed his eyes. When he opened them again he could see the bright orange flames of the fire, the heat warming his body. He closed them again and felt the world spin around him.

When he forced his eyes open he was falling, no, hanging over the water. He could see the boat below him. Nelson was on the deck holding a rope; his life line. Brad closed his eyes again, and this time he didn't try to open them.

He felt himself free falling then stop abruptly, the rope cutting in to his waist. Someone unclipped him from the line and laid him out on the deck. He felt himself being dragged back and propped against what he thought was the bridge.

Water hit his face and he willed his eyes open. He watched as Sean slid down the rope and hit the deck. The top of the platform was an inferno. The second deck was igniting and slowly starting to catch fire as the flames spread down. Brad rolled to his stomach and tried to stand but fell.

Chelsea hurried to his side. "Relax! Don't move."

Brad's body ached, but he forced himself into a sitting position and rested against the bridge. He looked up again and focused on the far away dock. The dock was empty now; the mob had left long ago to attack the stairway. Brooks revved the engines and the boat began to back away as Brad looked at the platform and tried to focus. He was there, the Alpha leader; he was standing at the edge of the dock with the platform burning all around him. They locked eyes just as the rest of the rig was swallowed in flames.

19.

Brad came to in a dark space. *Where the hell am I?* He started to panic and tried to sit up, hitting his head on the ceiling above him. Then he heard the hum of the diesel engines. He slowly began to remember the fight, and lying on the deck of the boat. Brad reached for a flashlight in his hip pocket. *What the ... Where are my clothes?*

Brad felt his body; he was dressed in nothing but his boxers and a T-shirt. He rolled to the side and reached along the floor. He found his bag and rifled through the front pockets, finding what he was searching for. He pulled the surefire flashlight from the pack's pocket and clicked it on.

He shone the light around the space. As he suspected, he was in the berthing compartment, or the barracks of the boat as he liked to think of it. Brad panned the light around the space. He saw Tony and Nelson sleeping on racks across from him. Looking farther down the compartment past a few racks filled with supplies, he saw Chelsea.

Brad rolled out of the bunk and put his feet on the floor. He felt groggy, but couldn't find any obvious injuries outside of a bad headache and a burning face. Brad ducked and stood in the center of the compartment. He found his boots next to the bag and slipped them on, then used the light to lead him out of the bow and stepped up the ladder to the bridge.

He opened the hatch and walked onto the bridge, where he found Brooks sitting in a large chair behind the steering controls. Sean was in a corner with a cup of coffee in his hand. He looked up, saw Brad, and smiled. "How ya feeling buddy?" he asked.

"Like shit; I have a killer headache and my face feels sunburned," Brad answered.

"You probably have a concussion, and you got some decent flash burns to your face, but you'll live," Brooks said.

Brad walked through the bridge and took an empty seat. "How long was I out?" he asked.

Sean poured Brad a cup of coffee and walked across the bridge to hand it to him. "About four hours. We should be at the island in another twelve."

"What about the air crew?" Brad asked.

"They are probably on the ground about now."

"What! Alone and in the dark?" Brad said, a worried look on his face.

"Well, we didn't have much of a choice with the platform gone and all. They flew ahead. But they won't be landing at the airfield. They are going to go in from an isolated corner of the island and try to find a place to hold up."

"Good, I was worried. Do we have comms with them?" Brad asked.

"We did, but they are out of range now. When we get closer I'll call for them. Everything is under control, Brad," Sean said.

Brad stood from the chair with the coffee in his hand. "Is it safe to go outside?"

"Yeah, have at it; just stay on the back deck. As a matter of fact, I'll join you," Sean said.

Sean walked to the compartment door and opened it, letting in the cool night air. He turned, walked toward the back deck, and sat his coffee cup atop one of the pallets of ammo. Brad followed him and did the same thing, then looked up to marvel at the bright moon and sky full of stars.

"It's amazing isn't it? Nothing better than a star-filled sky when you're far out to sea," Sean said.

"It's something else. At least that's one thing that hasn't changed."

"You feel that, Brad?" Sean asked him.

"Feel what?"

"That." Sean paused. "The feeling of security. No primals out here, buddy; those damn things can't swim. We're safe at sea."

"What happened on the platform seemed like a deliberate attack. They actually opened the purge valves?" Brad asked him.

"Brad, if you would have told me a week ago they were capable of planning, I would have said you were full of shit. But the evidence is stacking up. I don't know what to think of it. For starters, we obviously need to step up our game."

"I saw the Alpha on the dock as we pulled away; he was staring right at me."

"What? I don't know, man; you were pretty far out of it when we pulled out. Either way though, that goose is cooked."

"For sure, we can't afford to lose anyone else." Brad shook his head and looked down at his feet. "Chief, I think I'm going to try and grab a few more z's. If you or Brooks need me to relieve you, wake me up."

"Okay buddy, get some rest," Sean said.

Brad got to his feet and made his way back inside the bridge. He placed his coffee cup on the console in front of Brooks and repeated his offer to give him a break. Brooks said he was good to go, and that Brad should try to relax a bit after the fall he took. Brad nodded and made his way back into the berthing compartment.

He shined the light around the space and found everyone still sleeping soundly. Brad kicked off his boots and lay back down on his tiny bunk. He only had maybe a foot of space as the top bunk filled with supplies hung just above his chest, but it still beat sleeping on the ground. He closed his eyes and tried to sleep but his mind wandered to Ryan, Ben, and Wilson. Brad rolled to the side and tried to think of happier days and let the engine's hum sing him to sleep.

Brad woke to the calming sounds of water slapping the side of the hull as he slowly opened his eyes. The compartment had heated up quite a bit, and there was light coming down from the ladder well. Brad got to his feet and dug through his bag until he found a clean uniform. He elected to leave the heavy jacket off and instead just wore the T-shirt. Brad climbed up the stairs and saw Tony sitting at the controls.

"Hey Brad, how are you this morning?" Tony asked.

"I'm good Tony, where are we?"

Tony pointed off the port side, far in the distance. "We're anchored just off the island while they peek around a bit." Tony changed his gaze toward the front of the ship.

Brad looked and could see the hazy outline of the island about a mile out. On the bow of the boat, he could see Brooks and Sean lying in the prone position behind their heavy rifles and spotting scopes. Brad nodded and thanked Tony. Seeing the coffee was still on, he poured himself a cup, then walked out toward the back deck. He found Nelson and Chelsea sitting on some benches eating a cold MRE breakfast.

"Morning, Sergeant. Hey, you want my pound cake? Stuff constipates me something fierce," Nelson said to Brad while holding up a small tan package.

"Well damn, Nelson, how could anyone pass it up with that sales pitch?" Brad said, smiling and taking the package from Nelson.

"How's your head, Brad?" Chelsea asked.

"It's fine. I think I just got my bell rung when the blast took me off my feet. I appreciate you all taking care of me last night," Brad answered as he peeled open the cake and dunked it into his coffee.

They heard the clop of boots and the rattle of equipment as the SEALs moved up behind them. Sean explained that there was no movement across the water on the island's pier. A few broken ships were tied up, apparently battered by the same cyclone that had hit them the week prior. Everything appeared to be good and quiet, at least out in the open.

"Brad, you up for a recon? We're looking to take the inflatable in close, possibly to the beach. We will do some quick sneak and peek. If it's all clear, Tony can bring in the boat," Sean said.

"I'm up for it. Have you heard from the air crew?"

"Talked to them about thirty minutes ago; they're tucked in to some high terrain south of the airfield, and so far, they haven't seen anything. Bradley said it's pretty barren from what they can see."

"Sounds like a good time. Give me a few minutes to suit up and I'll be ready to go."

20.

When Brad climbed back onto the deck, they already had the rigid inflatable sitting in the water with the front pulled up onto the dive deck. Brooks tossed Brad a small self-inflating life vest. "Make sure you wear your floaties. I don't wanna have to go pullin' your ass out of the drink," Brooks said with a smile.

Brad took the device and strapped it over his gear. He didn't even try to pretend like he knew how it worked, so Brooks gave him a quick rundown on the mechanics of it. Basically, if he fell out of the raft, it would quickly fill with air from compressed cartridges. "Nice to have when you are wearing seventy pounds of gear in a small rubber boat trying to break the surf," Brooks halfheartedly joked.

Sean positioned Brad in the front of the raft and took a position opposite him, while Brooks had the helm. The engine turned over easily and they slowly moved away from the boat's dive deck to head toward the shore. Sean got on the small radio and checked in with the boat and the Blackhawk crew. If they got into trouble, the Blackhawk could still provide air cover.

The water was calm and the raft easily cut through the short swells. Brad looked up at the sun, thinking it would be a hot one today. They were just off the coast of Oman and he knew this part of the world could easily hit over a hundred degrees in the daytime. For now it was nice and cool, and the movement of the boat was creating a pleasant ocean breeze. In another time and place, this would have been a relaxing day at the beach.

As the small raft slid through the water, they began to make out the harbor ahead of them. There were a number of docks farther south, and it appeared to be a civilian shipping port; judging by the ferry tied up and some larger shipping vessels. To the north, and closer to the air base, sat one long pier. A military vessel was positioned at the end of it. A large sandy cove was cut into the beach, with the mouth being next to the military pier.

Brooks turned the craft slightly and headed towards the cove. As the raft got closer, they could see that the military ship was in a state of disrepair; maybe it had even been salvaged. There were holes cut into the hull; the ship was covered in rust and flaking paint. Brooks slowly cruised the raft past it and turned into the mouth of the cove. The water flattened out and he cut the engine, allowing them to drift and listen for sounds of company.

The boat glided forward and hit the sand with a soft grinding sound. They sat quietly, listening to sea gulls squawk and the ocean waves lapping against the beach. Quickly dismounting the boat, Brad helped grab the handles as they dragged it ashore and tucked it next to a berm. Sean and Brooks then moved toward a small rise in the sand and dropped into the prone position. Brad followed their movements, staying just a step behind them.

Sean had his binoculars out and was panning them along the beach and surrounding areas. Just over the berm, they could make out a small Navy shipyard of sorts. There were some heavy lift vehicles, fuel trucks, and several large wet storage containers. The pier next to them also held vehicles and a few small buildings. Sean slowly got to his knees and pointed to the end of the pier. Brooks nodded and stepped off briskly in a light trot.

They moved parallel to the beach, using the berm as cover to conceal them from the shipyard. Once Brooks reached the pier, Sean and Brad moved in behind him. The pier rose about ten feet above the water and was made entirely of stone and earth, with the surface being poured concrete. Brooks moved towards the top of it and took up a concealed position while Sean and Brad ran past him and farther up the pier.

They reached the first vehicle: a large fuel truck. The truck's hoses were dragged out of the back and were hanging over the side of the pier. Brad moved around the truck and saw bullet holes in the windshield. The warm fuzzy feelings were starting to fade.

"Looks like someone topped off here and got the hell out of Dodge fast," Sean said.

"See those bullet holes?" Brad asked.

"Yup, maybe it was looters stealing fuel. Guards must have shot at them," Brooks said, slowly walking over.

"Looters, ha, you mean just like us?" Brad said.

"Yup, something like that," Brooks said as he inspected the truck. "This truck's tank is dry. Chief, you want to clear the entire pier or move inland?"

"Let's call up the boat; they can anchor in the cove near the raft while we search for fuel. That should help keep them hidden," Sean answered.

Sean called Tony on the radio and gave him direction to the cove. Soon they saw the boat's profile as it drew closer to the shore. Tony was moving slowly to keep the boat as quiet as possible. It moved around the pier and into the cove before Tony cut the engines. Nelson and Swanson were out on deck, dropping anchor lines and tying them off.

From Brad's angle, he was amazed by the image of the attack boat. He'd thought it looked large before, but it really was intimidating as well, with its large, sharp lines and grey, tiger-striped pattern. With the large cannon on the bow and the machine guns on the deck, it was a lot to take in. Too bad the primals couldn't be scared off.

Sean conversed with Tony over the radio, letting him know they would be searching for fuel, and planned to be back within the hour. This quick field trip was only to find fuel. The boat was already well provisioned, but they would need diesel for the boat and JP-8 for the Blackhawk to make it to Socotra Island.

Brooks led the way, with Sean and Brad walking behind him. It felt good to be off of the platform and once again on solid ground. The pier was connected to a road that led farther inland, but also split off toward a gated compound. A sign in both Arabic and English indicated it was the *tank farm*. They followed the road toward the high fences and found a gate.

The gates were cracked open, and destroyed padlocks hung from their locks. Brad helped Brooks pull the gates open. The entrance to the tank farm held two small guard shacks, which they cautiously approached and found empty. The small block buildings were intact, but the windows had all been broken out. There were several signs of a struggle in and around the guard shacks.

Brooks continued forward until he spied a parking lot with a number of vehicles lined up. Toward the back, they found four large fuel trucks and a couple of maintenance vehicles. They patrolled in that direction, moving quietly and wary of any movement. They set up a mini-perimeter around the first fuel truck which had DIESEL painted on its side. Sean opened the cab door carefully and inspected the interior, while Brooks jumped to the back of the truck and opened a hatch to the vehicle's tank. It was over three-quarters full, plenty to top off the attack boat. Upon inspecting the other three trucks, they found them also full of diesel. Brad had heard that a Blackhawk could fly on diesel, but he was sure Captain Bradley wouldn't be happy about it. Hoping to find more, Brooks pushed forward toward the tank yard.

They passed a large fuel point where several pumps and fuel lines were connected to a long string of pipes – exactly what they were looking for. A number of them were labeled as petrol and JP-8. Sean checked out the pumps and found them operational. Although there was no power, an emergency pump on the end appeared to be gravity-fed. It would take longer, but should work for the pilots.

Brooks spotted a large guard tower and took to the high ground to provide security while they ran the refueling operations. Brad jumped into the cab of the large diesel refueler to start it, but the truck refused to turn over. They tried the other trucks; however, they also had dead batteries. Sean dug though the maintenance tow vehicle and found a starter cart with four, twelve-volt batteries strapped to it.

Quickly they pulled the cart to the nearest fuel truck, and married the cart's batteries to the truck's engine compartment. Brad jumped back in the cab and pushed the start button. The truck clicked, groaned, and then roared to life. Sean pulled the cart out of the way and ran to the back of the truck, jumping onto the bumper. Brad ground the truck into gear and pulled forward out of the gate and headed toward the beach.

He could see the top of the boat sticking above the berm, and Nelson running across the bow deck, readying the boat for the fuel truck's arrival. Swanson and Nelson pulled the anchors and Tony guided the boat next to the pier just as Brad eased alongside of it. Sean quickly jumped out and pulled several feet of fuel line from a reel mounted on the rear of the truck.

Swanson took the other end and connected it to the boat's tanks. She gave the ready signal and Sean turned a wheel, releasing fuel to the boat. As they waited to top off the boat's tanks, Sean called the air crew and gave them directions to the tank farm and indicated where they would need to land the bird. They all knew the helicopter would make some noise and possibly bring in unwanted attention, so the timing had to be perfect.

Sean and Brad jumped out of the truck, leaving Nelson and Swanson to finish the refueling. They ran back to the tank farm and pulled a long hose out and away from the fuel point. Sean connected one end to the JP-8 spout and opened the valve. He watched the hose stiffen and he quickly shut the valve back off.

"Brooks, how's it looking up there?" Sean called over his radio.

"All clear Boss, the airbase is looking like a ghost town," Brooks answered.

"Roger that, I'm going to call in the bird and get things refueled. Be ready to move back to the beach as soon as it lifts off," Sean relayed back.

Sean radioed the air crew and gave them the go. Within five minutes, they could hear the whooping of its blades. Just as Sean had asked, they came in from over the ocean instead of flying across the island. Bradley flew the helicopter low and fast. Staying low helped conceal the exact location of the helicopter as it approached the tank farm. The bird touched down in a huge cloud of dust. Sean and Brad turned their backs to the helicopter until it was powered down and the blades stopped spinning.

As soon as it was stopped, Craig and Mr. Douglas jumped out and ran for the fuel nozzles. Mr. Douglas connected the fuel hose and gave Sean the thumbs up. Sean spun the wheel, opening the valve, and watched the hose stiffen as it filled with fuel. Mr. Douglas had told them they should be done in less than ten minutes. Sean received a call from the boat team that they had finished filling the tanks and were anchored back in the cove.

Brad had moved away and was providing security near the maintenance trucks when Mr. Douglas yelled that all of the tanks were topped off, and for Sean to cut the fuel off. Sean spun the wheel and shut off the fuel feed. He then watched as Mr. Douglas disconnected the nozzle and handed it to Craig, who pulled the hose away from the helicopter.

"We are all set here, Chief. Get clear and we can get airborne," Captain Bradley yelled from the cockpit.

Brooks leaned out of the tower and yelled, "We got company!"

"Primals? How many?" Sean yelled back.

"Nope, these look a tad bit more dangerous. I got two vehicles: a jeep and an open-back truck, ten, maybe fifteen men."

"Captain, hold off on the engines but be ready to go on my word," Sean said as he walked past the bird. He met up with Brad and together they slowly walked towards the tank farm's gate to greet the visitors.

21.

As they casually walked toward the gate's entrance, Sean continued to communicate with Brooks, who was lying prone on the tower's catwalk. Brooks had hidden himself in the shadows with his suppressed M14, and his radio headset was perfectly synched with Sean's.

"Keep eyes on them. Be ready to cover us. You prioritize your targets," Sean calmly said into the radio.

"You expecting trouble, Chief?" Brad asked as they walked to the center of the lane and watched the two vehicles drive around the corner.

"Not expecting, Brad, just preparing for it. Stay frosty and let me do the talking. Be prepared to react."

The jeep pulled through the gate and stopped nearly twenty-five feet from where Brad and Sean were standing. The truck drove beyond the jeep and parked on the far side. Both vehicles were clearly marked as Oman military. The vehicles looked to be in good working order. Not combat ready, though. Brad thought they looked like security forces, possibly airport police.

The soldiers jumped from the back of the open-topped truck and formed up around the side. They were standing in more of a gaggle than a military formation. Brad carefully watched the group of men. They didn't have the mannerisms of professionals. They joked and held their rifles carelessly; even more alarming, they were not uniformly dressed. Some wore tennis shoes; one soldier was even in sandals. *'Maybe these men are contract security?'* Brad thought to himself.

Two men in military uniform climbed out of the jeep, one a tall, dark-skinned man with an African complexion, and the other a smaller, possibly Persian, man. Neither of them, nor the soldiers for that matter, appeared to be of Middle Eastern descent. Brad's internal warning bells began to chime.

The African man walked with the swagger that identified him as the one in charge. He spoke privately to the smaller man. The two pretended not to see Brad and Sean as they took their time walking back to the truck and speaking with their men. There was a great deal of laughing as the men nodded their heads in agreement with the man in charge.

"Looks like we may be dealing with some arrogance, no telling who these fools are," Sean whispered. "Just stay casual, hands off your weapons."

After several minutes, the two presumed officers turned, as if they had just noticed the presence of the uniformed Americans and the large helicopter sitting in front of them. The presumed leader turned and said something to the smaller man and they both laughed. They began strolling towards Brad and Sean. Brad saw that only the shorter man carried a rifle. The tall man had a holstered pistol.

Brad noticed that the tall man was wearing a mix of uniforms. He had on a Saudi uniform jacket, with American-style MultiCam pants. His cover looked like an airline pilot's cap, or maybe a ship's captain's hat. He was wearing the railroad track insignia that would identify him as an Army captain. The other man's uniform was better put together, but it was of a completely different pattern and appeared to be an enlisted man's rank.

They stopped about eight paces away. They continued speaking to each other as if Brad and Sean were not there. The shorter man belted out an exaggerated laugh. Then the tall man locked eyes with Sean and spoke in a stern voice. Sean calmly shrugged his shoulders and showed the palms of his hands, indicating he did not understand the man's language.

The man shook his head. "Of course ... Americans. You never bother to learn another language. Is this better for you?" the tall man said.

"Oh yes, thank you, that's much better. How can we help you gentleman?" Sean answered.

At this both men let out another exaggerated laugh. "Help us ... You are a funny American. You are stealing from us. You have stolen fuel and who knows what else."

"Oh come on, pal. You know what is going on in the world. We are just borrowing some fuel and we will be on our way. I'll write you a receipt and I'm sure you will receive payment from Uncle Sam."

The men laughed again. Brad looked beyond the men and saw that the band of the soldiers had spread out and were holding their rifles nervously.

The tall man stepped forward and shook his head in disappointment. "I am sorry, but we must place you under arrest; and I will have to confiscate your helicopter, and its crew."

"Oh is that so? Damn, this is just turning out to be a horrible day for me. I was hoping we would be able to work this out. So who is it again that's arresting me?" Sean asked.

Brad watched the men in the back closely. They had stopped moving and seemed to feel confident that they had the Americans trapped. They began to step closer, then halted again when they were less than fifteen feet away.

"I am General Osman; I am in command of this entire base and island. Now you will surrender your weapons to me," the tall man said in a stern voice.

Sean used his hands to mockingly straighten his uniform, then looked back at the man, smiling. "Oh no way, shucks. My bad, General, the captain's rank on your pirate uniform threw me for a spin there. I went and got all confused." Sean stopped speaking for a second, then brought his eyes to the ground and shook his head from side to side. When he looked back up, he gave the general a serious stare.

"You know what? Fuck it; I'm too tired for this horseshit today. See, I don't know how you managed to put yourself in command. But I'm going to ask you really nice-like to turn around and go back to where you came from. All we need is a few minutes and you can have this island all to yourselves again."

The man was obviously shocked. He spoke rapidly to the short man next to him. Brad didn't understand the words, but he could tell that the tall man was frustrated and not used to having his orders ignored.

The general scowled. "I am going to give you a count of five, then my men will execute you. This will be your last warning. You are under arrest," the tall man again demanded.

"Well darn. I was really hoping that it wouldn't come to this …. Brooks you still on? Yeah, this isn't going well … Go ahead and take the short fat man …" Sean said.

"Wait … who is this Brooks?" the fake general demanded.

There was a muffled pop and a zip through the air as a high speed projectile passed between Brad and Sean and smacked the short man in the middle of the forehead. The short man stood with a blank expression for a few seconds, then fell over and onto his back. The fake general was in shock. Brad watched as the man's arrogance turned to fear. He took a single step backwards, then looked back at Sean.

"This is an outrage, now my men will …"

Sean interrupted the man and spoke into the radio.

"Yeah, Brooks, the tall one next, yeah that's right … the one with the captain's bars on his uniform."

"No, no, no, wait, wait," the man pleaded with Sean as he took another step back. "We can negotiate, we can negotiate."

"Hmmm, hey Brooks, give me a second, buddy. Sounds like the general wants to negotiate, just hang tight okay?"

Brad looked back at the armed soldiers ... or were they pirates? They all looked confused, as if they didn't know what to do when they were off their game plan. Brad guessed they hadn't come across this situation before. They were probably used to robbing civilians and the random merchant that came into port looking for fuel, and had never been challenged before.

Sean stepped forward and placed his hands on his hips. "So, here's how this negotiation will work. You and your men will turn around and leave."

"Come on friend, you can at least compensate us for the fuel and the death of my man."

"Okay ... That offer is now off the table. Offer two is this. You drop your weapons now. Turn around and drive through that gate. You have to the count of ten, or we kill all of you," Sean said, losing patience.

"You shoot me!" the general shouted. "No, I shoot on you! I have many men with rifles! They will skin you alive! I have many more in the barracks. You have *one* hidden man with a rifle," the fake general said, losing his temper.

"General ... Captain, Pirate ... or whatever you want to be called today. See that helicopter behind me? That is a chain gun hanging out of that window. If you would care to look behind you in the harbor, that pretty boat there has a mounted 30-millimeter cannon. And yes, let's not forget my trained friend who just happens to be so good with his rifle he could kill all of your men on his own. Now what's it going to be, Pirate?" Sean said.

The general locked eyes with Sean and gave an angry stare. He slowly reached into his holster and pulled a small revolver out. He dropped the small hand gun near the body of the short man. "Very well, you have ten minutes, then I come back," the fake general said.

The tall man turned around and faced the other men and began yelling at them. They scrambled, looked confused, dropped their rifles, and ran back to the trucks. The tall man walked back and sat in the jeep as the engines started and they pulled through the gate.

"We need to hurry. Captain Bradley, get that bird fired up. Brooks, back to the boat now," Sean yelled.

The Blackhawk began whining and the blades picked up speed. Soon they were whipping, kicking up a cloud of dust. Sean ran to the pilot's seat and spoke with Captain Bradley. He closed the cockpit door and ran back to Brad. Brooks pulled up behind them; his MP5 was still slung and he carried the large M14 at the ready.

They stepped off quickly with Sean leading the way. The Blackhawk lifted off the ground and flared back, intentionally causing a large cloud of dust and sand to screen the back drop of the running men. The helicopter gained altitude and turned, heading out to sea and taking a path directly over the attack boat.

Sean was the first to reach the top berm. Just as he got there, they heard the first reports of automatic weapons fire coming at them from the base. "Yup, right on time. Guys like that can never leave well enough alone," Sean said.

They ran and dove behind the berm as poorly placed shots hit the sand around them. Brad dared to peek over the berm and could see a small armored car and several men moving in their direction. There was a pirate on a 12.7-millimeter gun in the armored car's turret. The rounds were skipping off the ground and flying over the attack boat. Brooks dropped to his belly and brought up his rifle. A single round discharged and the pirate on the gun dropped back into the vehicle.

Brooks and Brad ran for the inflatable and dragged it back into the water. Sean was crouched low, walking behind them and talking into the radio as more rounds began to explode into the top of the berm once the armored vehicle's gunner was replaced.

The 30-millimeter gun on the fast attack boat's deck opened up and launched high explosive projectiles at the armored car. Brad heard the *crack, crack, crack* of the rounds smacking the ground, then the *whoomp* and secondary explosion of a hit on the armored car.

Brad leapt into the boat behind Sean just as Brooks started the engine. He held onto the side of the inflatable as Brooks raced it forward and made a quick lap around the attack boat. Brooks cut the boat hard and revved the engine; they drove fast and flew up the dive deck.

Sean tossed a line to Swanson, who quickly tied the inflatable off to the deck. The large boat's engine roared and turned in the water. As the attack boat changed direction, the forward-looking deck gun was taken off line; Sean and Brooks stepped up to the fifty caliber machine guns on the back deck and continued to place suppressing fire on the pirates, who were now spread out but still firing.

The boat picked up speed and quickly raced away from the beach and back into open water. The SEALs stopped firing and focused their attention on strapping down the inflatable. Sean took a headcount and verified everyone was okay before he walked to the raft and lifted out his gear.

"What a bunch of assholes. The world is falling apart and we still have people wanting to kill us ... and for what ... a helicopter that those fucktards can't even fly?" Sean said, shaking his head. "Tony, make our course towards Socotra please, and check in with the bird. Let them know we are enroute."

"On it, Chief," Tony shouted back.

22.

The vessel leveled out at a smooth thirty knots; Brad was still on the back deck looking over the side. He had stripped down to his T-shirt and was enjoying the view. They had decided to follow the coast south to the island of Socotra. He could see the shore far in the distance, a tan outline of the desert coast. The sun was shining hot on the deck but the ocean's spray was cool and comforting.

Brad moved to a bench near the back dive deck and sat down. He pulled his Oakley's down over his eyes and laid his head back. Brooks was at the controls now. Brad heard the hatch close and looked up to see Tony make his way back onto the deck. "Mind if I take a seat?" Tony yelled over the roar of the engines.

Brad nodded to him, and the older man sat at the opposite end of the bench. Tony reached into his pocket and fetched a cigarette. Cupping his hand from the stiff breeze, he lit the end and took a long drag.

"Best thing about being off of that platform, I can finally smoke in the open again," Tony said.

"That's the best thing? I think I'll go with not having things trying to attack and eat me twenty-four-seven," Brad shouted back.

Tony pulled the cigarette from his mouth and laughed. "Ha ha! Yeah, you're right; I think I'd like to change my answer."

They both laughed together. "You know a fishing pole and a case of beer would make this the perfect trip. I was kind of hoping to have time to track one down back at the last stop; a fishing pole, I mean," Tony smiled.

Brad nodded in agreement and settled into the bench, letting the sun's rays warm his face. "How long is it to Socotra?" he asked.

"Well if we can maintain thirty, I'd say we should be there in a good fifteen hours."

"And the Blackhawk?"

"It won't take them long at their speed. We're already out of radio range with them. This bucket only has a shitty HF radio and we only got about twenty-five miles range. They will be getting to the island in daylight, so hopefully they can find a nice safe place to hide," Tony explained.

"Unless the stories are true and the Navy is parked there waiting with welcoming arms," Brad said, smiling.

"Yup, unless that happens. Well I'm going to go scrounge up some food in the galley, you take it easy Brad," Tony said as he snuffed his cigarette and threw it into the breeze.

Brad sat enjoying the sun for a few minutes longer before he got up and entered the bridge, where he found Brooks sitting at the controls, leaning forward in deep concentration. Brooks looked back and noticed that he was being observed. He slapped the controls again and shook his head.

"Something wrong?" Brad asked.

"Nahh, just the damn GPS won't lock the way I want it to. Nothing to worry about, though. Our destination is a straight shot. We can pretty much follow the coast and run into it," Brooks answered.

"You picked up any radio traffic?" Brad asked.

"Nope, not a thing; I thought maybe closer to the shore we would at least get a radio station but, then again, this isn't exactly a popular spot on the planet. Maybe as we get closer to the island."

Brad took an empty seat next to Brooks and looked through the windscreen at the front of the bow to watch the open ocean of the unchanging scenery. Brad stood to look at a map of the region showing the penciled-in lines of their route that Sean and Brooks had drawn. They had a long way to go just to hit the island. He looked at a cutout on the corner of the map and could see that the region was very small when placed on an overlay of the globe. *How would they ever make it home?* he thought.

A number of different panels were bolted to the dash of the bridge. He could identify some of them from his times fishing on the Great Lakes, but others were a mystery to a ground-pounding soldier. Brad moved around looking at them, and saw what appeared to be a radar screen, almost like the emulated one he had seen in the tower. He asked Brooks if he could show him how it worked.

Brooks poked at the screen, showing how to identify objects and how to distinguish surface anomalies from actual targets. "What's that there?" Brad asked, pointing at two very small blips on the radar screen.

Brooks looked closer. He pressed buttons and tuned the radar. Two small green objects were moving on an intercept course with their vessel.

"You know, I'm not sure, but judging from the speed and because they are in a pair ... I would wager a guess that they are military aircraft," Brooks said, still turning dials. "Brad, would you mind fetching the chief for me?"

Brad ran below and found Sean passed out in one of the bunks. After rousing him, Brad told him what they had seen on the radar, causing Sean to swing out of bed and quickly join them on the bridge.

"What do you got, Brooks?" Sean asked.

"Looks like a couple of aircraft; definitely fast movers. They are on an intercept course with us. I don't think it's a coincidence that they are coming right at us."

"Change your heading; take us straight out to sea away from the coast. And full speed," Sean said.

Brooks moved back to his seat at the controls and turned the ship ninety degrees away from the coast they had been following. Once the turn was complete, he pushed the throttle all the way forward. The diesel engines roared and the bow rose up out of the water as the speed of the boat almost doubled. They quickly sped away and out of view of the coast.

Brad stood looking at the radar screen, watching the two objects slowly change course and stay on them. The rest of the crew had climbed up from the bow and joined them on the deck to ask what was going on and why the hasty maneuvers.

"Go ahead and take the speed back down and return to course, Brooks. Whatever they are, we won't outrun them and they're obviously tracking us," Sean ordered.

Brooks pushed the throttle back down and turned the boat until it was back on the GPS heading before he looked back at the radar.

"At this speed and heading, Chief, we should have a visual at any minute."

Sean opened the door to step out onto the deck just as two jet aircraft flying low and fast blew over them. Two quick blurs, and the roar of their engines filled the bridge.

"All stop Brooks, see if you can get them on the radio," Sean yelled.

The jets flew past at low altitude and banked together, circling around. They were now easily identified as US F\A-18 fighter aircraft. They had slowed in speed and appeared to float in the air as they made another pass. Sean took the radio from Brooks, but before he could speak the speakers came alive.

"Unidentified vessel, unidentified vessel, this is US Navy Aircraft Echo Two Seven, please identify yourself."

With the sound of the radio, everyone on the deck started celebrating and high fiving. They had finally made contact with the outside world, and not only that, but a world that was still capable of putting fighter aircraft into the sky. Sean smiled but put his hand up, asking for silence.

"This is Chief Petty Officer Rogers of the United States Navy on a commandeered Pakistani-flagged vessel. Requesting assistance," Sean said into the handset.

"Roger that Chief, we have been looking for you, we picked up your helicopter crew about an hour ago."

"Picked up? Is everyone okay?"

"Everyone is fine, Chief; Captain Bradley sends you his greetings. Chief ... Please adjust your heading twenty degrees east and wait for instructions."

"Roger, can do," Sean called back over the radio as Brooks pulled the controls to make the course corrections.

23.

    The entire crew was packed on the bridge. Sean had a set of heavy binoculars scanning the horizon. They had just begun to pick up multiple objects on the radar screen. Other than the occasional call on the radio for a course correction, they had not received any new details. Sean directed Brooks to maintain course and speed.
    Slowly a fleet came into view out of the haze. Brad could make out a number of objects on the horizon: large steel bodies topped with huge masts. He was not familiar with Navy vessels, so a ship was still just a ship to him. Brooks, on the other hand, had begun to get excited and started calling out the names and classes of different vessels. Brooks pointed to a carrier, appearing to stand tall and proud over the others.
    As they motored closer the radio came alive again. This time the order was to kill the engines and go dead in the water. Brooks cut the engine and the boat began bobbing in the calm seas. With the large ships on the horizon, the attack boat no longer felt very large to Brad. He opened the bridge door and stepped out onto the bow to take in the view.

Swanson and Nelson joined him on the front of the ship, marveling at the fleet in front of them. They could just barely make out a small Zodiac headed in their direction. A number of armed sailors were on the boat, along with a man standing behind a mounted machine gun. The sight didn't give Brad any second thoughts; he knew that was how he would do things if the roles were reversed.

The rigid-hulled Zodiac pulled up alongside them. The Zodiac's crew was dressed in digital blue camouflage with orange flotation devices, and the men were armed with M4s and shotguns. Still ten yards away, they called over a bull horn announcing their intentions to board. Sean was on the rear deck and asked them to toss him a line.

A man tossed Sean a rope and with the help of Nelson, they pulled the small boat in tight and tied it up to the attack craft. A man jumped on board and extended his hand to Sean.

"I'm Lieutenant Hanson; we're just going to process you all aboard, Chief. This shouldn't take long," the smiling young man said as he shook Sean's hand.

With the two boats secured together, the sailors boarded. They had asked for and received permission from Sean to do a quick search of the vessel. A doctor was with the boarding team and set up shop in the berthing compartment of the bow. One at a time he asked the crew of the attack boat to enter the compartment and strip naked. The doctor gave them a thorough inspection to make sure they were not infected.

When everyone had gone through the inspection process, Lieutenant Hanson asked the crew to have a seat on the aft deck of the attack boat while he called in the status of the crew and said they were ready for departure. Brad could only hear bits and pieces of the conversation, as Hanson was wearing an earpiece and it made it hard to follow what was happening.

Hanson stepped out of the bridge, smiling. "Okay everyone, looks like the doc has cleared you for arrival to the fleet. I'm sorry we don't have a lot of room, so I won't be allowing you to take any belongings onto the Zodiac. But don't worry, you will get everything back. And we'll be getting you out of those dirty uniforms."

Brad looked at himself for the first time. His uniforms were tired and worn, but still he had spent almost two months in the field with nothing more than a change of clothes. He wasn't sure if he should take the officer's comments as good news or an insult. Either way, it didn't sound like it was a point worth arguing.

Sean stepped up from his position on the bench and approached the officer. "Sir, you can have my dirty skivvies if that's what it takes. When will we be leaving?"

"Oh ... Sorry, Chief, you'll have to leave your weapons also," Hanson said, pointing to Sean's sidearms and the MP5 clipped to his gear.

Sean smiled at Hanson and leaned in close so the rest of the sailors couldn't hear. "Okay son, now you are just starting to sound stupid. I'm not about to surrender my weapons to you. I think you need to get back on that radio and make some calls," Sean said just above a whisper.

Brad watched as the lieutenant's facial expression changed from a smile to a look of concern. Hanson left the aft deck and casually walked onto the bridge, closing the door behind him. Sean strolled near the Zodiac and made casual conversation with the sailors. Chelsea shot Brad a concerned look and Brad responded with a shrug of his shoulders. He really didn't know how all of this would play out or how far Sean was willing to take it.

Hanson walked back out of the bridge, leaving the door open as he walked aft. Sean turned, smiling at him. "What's the word from the boss?" Sean asked.

"Good news, Chief. The skipper of the Barry says he will allow you all to bring on weapons and a basic supply of ammo, as long as you have a locker to secure them in."

"Great work Hanson, I knew you could do it," Sean replied.

Tony came forward and explained that there was a large tool box below that should hold everything. Hanson agreed, so they opened the engine room hatch and the sailors helped them bring the tool box out onto the deck. The crew, one at a time, verified that their weapons were clear as one of the sailors observed and then placed their weapons into the tool box.

With everything loaded in the box, Tony snapped its hatches shut and they loaded the box onto the Zodiac. Hanson quickly ushered everyone aboard.

"What happens with the attack boat now?" Brooks asked.

"Oh, it will become part of the fleet. You have a good amount of supplies on board; they will come in really handy,' Hanson said. "Don't worry; my guys will take good care of it."

They had all boarded the Zodiac with the exception of two sailors, who stayed on board the attack boat. They untied the line marrying them together before the engines came to life and the boats headed in the direction of the fleet. As they got closer, the attack boat peeled off and went away from the Zodiac.

Brad sat in the center of the Zodiac with Chelsea beside him. The small boat rode very rough in the water; plowing through swells. Brad bounced along and reached out to steady himself. As they drew closer to the vessel that he assumed would be their destination, Brad saw the number '52' stamped on the hull.

"52?" Brad asked no one in particular.

A sailor next to Brad turned around. "She is the DDG-52, the USS Barry," he said.

"What is it, some kind of battleship?"

The sailor laughed. "Nahh man, this is a destroyer!" the sailor said, with obvious pride in his voice.

The Zodiac pulled in close to the side of the large ship. Many men were on the deck tossing lines and shouting instructions to the Zodiac's crew, directing them toward the back. The crew quickly secured themselves and they rushed Brad and his friends onboard. Brad watched as a group of men brought the tool box aboard and sat it on the deck near them.

They found themselves sitting on a large helicopter landing pad, but the helicopter was missing. Brad knew they were on the back of the boat and that was about it. A group of officers also dressed in digital blue uniforms approached the group, but ignored everyone and walked directly to Sean. One of the officers stuck out his hand.

"Chief Rogers, welcome aboard," the man said.

"Thank you sir, good to be here," Sean answered.

"Good, good. I'm Commander Shepherd, the Executive Officer of the Barry. I wanted to greet you firsthand. I wish we had more time to talk right now, but we have protocols to follow for new arrivals," Shepherd said.

"Protocols?" Sean asked.

"Yeah, nothing to worry about. You are going to sit in a twenty-four hour quarantine. But don't sweat it, Chief. Enjoy the downtime, okay? Try and get some rest. I will be down to debrief you about this time tomorrow. Sorry I can't stay, but I am extremely busy today. Once again, welcome aboard," Shepherd said smiling, shaking Sean's hand again before walking away.

As the officer left, another man stepped forward. He was short and solidly built with a gold anchor on his collar. "I'm Master Chief Swan; I want to welcome you aboard. You have no gear so that will make this easy. I need you to follow the instructions of my masters at arms and follow them below. You will all have an opportunity to shower and clean yourselves up. We will provide you with appropriate rest, gear, and get you a clean rack and some hot chow for your bellies. I know you all have questions, but seriously, the sooner we start the clock on this quarantine, the sooner I can get you all out. So let's get moving."

Quickly a group of younger enlisted sailors stepped forward and ushered them into the ship. They were split into groups. Sean was quickly pulled aside by the master chief while Brad, Brooks, and Nelson were taken away by two men. They watched as Chelsea was led away by two females and Tony was taken in another direction by two other sailors.

They were led deep into the ship and down various passageways. Brad was quickly lost and didn't have a clue where he was. They were brought into a small compartment that looked like it might possibly be a workspace. The two sailors guided them into the room and asked them to sit down while they waited outside.

Brad took a seat across from Brooks and sat quietly. Nelson was sitting in a corner looking nervous and uncomfortable. "Relax brother, this is all part of the game," Brooks said to him.

A new face entered the room: a middle-aged tall black man, obviously enlisted by the way he carried himself. He introduced himself as a Navy corpsman and asked the men to remove their shirts. He dropped a small bag on a table and pulled out a number of syringes and vials. He walked up next to Brooks and readied the needle. Brooks quickly snapped up his hand and grabbed the corpsman by the wrist.

The two masters at arms men looked in the doorway with nervous stares.

"Would you mind telling me what this is before you just go sticking me with it?" Brooks said in a calm voice.

"I'm sorry; this is just a batch of antibiotics. The next is a host of antivirals. It will kill any crud you may have picked up and help keep you all from getting sick on the boat," the man said nervously.

"Oh cool, thanks for explaining that to me, Doc; proceed," Brooks said, letting go of the man's wrist.

The corpsman went around the room administering drugs. He left, and promptly their two escorts got them back to their feet and ushered them further down the passageway. They walked past a cage door where a female sailor handed them a pillowcase with two sheets, a pillow, a pair of ugly blue shorts, flip flops, and a yellow T-shirt.

Again they were led down a long passageway, ending up in what looked like a locker room. A man was waiting for them; he sat them in a chair one by one and shaved away the beards and unkempt hair. Then the escorts handed them a number of heavy Ziploc bags. They were instructed to dump all of their belongings into the bags and to strip naked and discard their uniforms into a large, black plastic trash bag.

Brad placed everything from his pockets into the bag and started to seal it. He stopped, pulled his unit patch and the American flag off his uniform, and added them to the Ziploc. Then he stripped down to his boxers and sat back on the bench. One of the escorts looked at Brad and shook his head. "All the way naked, Sergeant," he said.

Brad shook his head and stripped off and tossed his boxers into the bag. "Damn Navy meat gazers," he joked to Nelson.

Nelson laughed and stripped down next, then stood and thrust his hips at the sailor. "Am I naked enough for you seamen?" he laughed.

"Okay, that's enough," Brooks said to the two of them, trying not to crack up himself.

The bag of soiled uniforms was taken away and they were led around a corner and instructed to shower. When finished, they dressed in the Navy athletic uniforms, which made them all, except Brooks, feel very awkward. The two escorts again led them down a hall and into another room.

This room had two sets of bunk beds and a table in the center. The table held trays of food and a pitcher of water. The escort informed them that they would have to stay in the room for twenty-four hours under observation. If they needed anything they should pound on the door. Then he stepped back into the passage way and closed the door, locking it behind him.

24.

Brooks walked across the room and tossed his bag onto a mattress. "I call bottom rack," he said.

"Yeah, me too," said Brad as he tossed his onto the other bottom mattress.

"Cool, I got top!" Nelson said with fake enthusiasm.

Brooks sat down at the table and pulled a tray close to him. He took a scoop of the food, slowly tasted it, and feigned a thoughtful expression before he shoveled down the rest. Brad and Nelson followed suit. Soon the food was gone and the pitcher empty.

Brad walked across the room to fill the pitcher from a faucet. They were lucky to have the rare berthing space equipped with a working head and running water. Almost like a prison cell. There was barely any water pressure, but it was enough. He sat back down and set the pitcher on the table. He saw that Nelson had already climbed onto a top rack and was snoring away on his pillowcase full of bedding.

"Damn kid didn't even take the time to make his bed!" Brad laughed, pointing.

"Yeah, but he's got the right idea," Brooks said as he pulled the bedding from his bag and stretched it across the mattress.

"Where do you think Captain Bradley and the air crew are at?" Brad asked Brooks.

"Don't know, man, I'm thinking maybe they made it to the island? Or possibly they landed on one of the boats. Your guess is as good as mine. I'm sure Chief will find out."

"Yeah, hopefully we find out a lot more tomorrow. I think it's strange, you know, finding a fleet just parked here in the middle of nowhere. Shit, you would think they would be hauling ass home."

"Yeah maybe. But I'm glad they were here. You mind hitting the lights. I'm ready to check out for a while."

Brad nodded and finished making his bed before walking across the room and shutting off the lights. He made his way back to his rack and lay awake, staring at the bunk above him. He could already hear Brooks snoring and Nelson was tossing about but still sleeping heavily.

They were safe, he should be able to rest now, but something still didn't feel right. Brad tried to clear his thoughts and make his mind blank so he could sleep, but his mind continued to wander. He thought of the men he'd left behind in the compound. He wondered if Hassan was okay back in the village where they had last seen him. Too many things. He closed his eyes and tried again to clear his thoughts.

There was a clicking at the door as someone used a key on the other side to unlock it. The door lock mechanism clanked and the handle turned. The door squeaked open and someone flipped on the lights. Brad lifted his head from under a heavy green blanket. He saw one of the young escorts had replaced the trays on the table with new trays filled with eggs, while another man placed a fresh pitcher of water on the table.

Brad rolled over and pulled the blanket over his head. He heard a third man enter the room and water was poured into a drinking glass. The third man dismissed the two guards and asked them to close the door. Brad heard the door close, but he could still hear movement in the room.

Brad rolled over in his rack and saw a man sitting at the table. He was wearing a blue button-down shirt and black rimmed glasses. He was skinny with a pointy head. The man looked up at Brad.

"Good morning," he said.

"Umm, is it morning already?" Brad said, slowly easing himself out of the rack.

"Well ... actually early afternoon. Almost eleven a.m.," the man said. "I trust you all slept well. No problems?"

"No, we're fine ... Who are you?" Brad asked, forcing himself into a sitting position. Brad stood and walked to the latrine. He relieved himself as he waited for the man to answer.

"My name is Mr. John Smith," the man answered.

Brooks lifted himself from the mattress and sat up stretching; he let a big yawn then smiled. "Mr. Smith, aye? Not really original is it?" Brooks said with a grin.

"Well anyhow, since I'm not going to get your name; why are you here, Mr. Smith?" Brad said as he walked back to the table and sat down.

Mr. Smith said he was their debrief officer. Brad listened to him explain things as he slid a tray across the table and took in a heaping fork full of eggs. "Damn man, powdered eggs. Not cool," Brad scowled. "Hey, do you know where Captain Bradley and the rest of our people are at?" Brad asked.

"They are fine, Sergeant; they landed on the island," Mr. Smith answered.

"The island? Then why didn't we go there?" Brad asked.

"Just a matter of convenience. We would have directed them here as well, but they made it to the island before we could intercept them."

"Intercept, aye ... Doesn't sound too friendly," Brad said, grinning.

"Sorry, the island has been designated a safe zone. Under normal conditions, no one is allowed entry until quarantined and debriefed. The admiral spent a lot of resources clearing the island. We would like to keep it that way," Mr. Smith explained.

"That's why you brought us here then?" Brooks asked.

"That's correct; your Captain Bradley was flying low and fast over the water. We didn't pick him up until he was already on approach. And by that time he refused to change heading and landed on the island. No harm though, they're going through a similar process at the airbase."

Nelson woke and jumped from his rack. "Hey, you guys didn't tell me chow was here. Who is this?" he asked, pointing at the skinny man.

"He is the man whose name we dare not speak," Brooks blurted out laughing.

Nelson laughed along, "Oh cool, well nice to meet ya then." Nelson took a tray and began eating.

"Anyhow, each of you will be debriefed by a member of our team. Nothing to be concerned with; just basic information. Where your unit was located. What you remember about the fall. If you know the names and locations of any other survivors," Mr. Smith said.

Nelson started to ramble, as he took a bite of rehydrated sausage. Mr. Smith quickly cut him off and said they would be debriefed individually; this now was just an introduction. Mr. Smith stood from the table and stepped toward the door. "Finish your breakfast. Your presence will be requested shortly," Mr. Smith said as he knocked on the door and was let out by the guards.

"And the fun begins," Brooks said as he grabbed the glass of water and drank it down. "Don't worry about that guy, he's either a shrink or a spook, nothing to worry about. Just be honest with him and ask a shit ton of questions."

There was a quick knock at the door. The female sailor that had issued them the bedding a day earlier entered with three partially-filled sea bags. She sat them on the table and handed each of the men a form that she required they sign. She said very little, and once she received the signatures she left the room.

"Chatty gal, that one," Nelson joked.

The uniforms they were given were Navy issue, but not the blue type. They were of a tan desert pattern. Brad didn't really care what they looked like as long as the boots fit, and was happy to find that they did. He removed his Ziploc bag and placed the personal items back in his pockets, then he attached the Velcro unit patch and the flag on his sleeve.

Brad stood to look in the mirror. He laughed. "Damn, I look like shit. Must have lost about twenty pounds."

"We all have buddy, we all have," Brooks answered.

The door opened again and one of the escorts walked in the room.

"Sergeant Thompson, Mister Smith is ready for you," the guard said.

"Well shucks, don't want to leave him waiting," Brad said as he moved towards the door.

25.

Brad was led through the passageway, down stairs, and around corners. He felt like he had been brought lower in the ship, but it was hard for him to tell. Eventually they stopped at a stateroom door. The room appeared to be a dorm room of sorts, and the guard pounded on the door before opening it. Mr. Smith was sitting at a desk; Brad was directed to a chair next to the bunk.

The man quickly asked Brad a list of generic questions: Name, social, home of record. The questions went on and on. He asked where Brad had been stationed during the fall; the names of as many people as he could remember from his unit; the disposition of this unit. The man asked Brad to tell his story in detail. During parts of the story, he would stop Brad to ask questions. He wrote everything down in a spiral note book.

When Mr. Smith finished, he sat the notebook on a desk and offered Brad a cup of coffee. While Brad sipped at the coffee, Mr. Smith went through the notes, flipping the pages of his notebook while making marks on the paper. After an uncomfortable silence, the questions began again. Often the information was a repeat of earlier answers, asking for more elaboration.

The time spent in the room was exhausting. Finally the man offered Brad a refill of his cup and asked if he had any questions of his own.

"Well sir, my mind feels like it is going to explode, but right off the bat, is there a plan to get the rest of my people home?"

The man looked at Brad seriously before answering. "Sergeant, honestly, we have heard sporadic reports of survivors across the globe. Some we have even verified by satellite or drone. But as of today, recovery missions are very rare. Our resources are scarce, so no. I mean I cannot say for certain that it will not happen. But I wouldn't count on it."

"There has got to be something we can do. All we need is an aircraft and we can get them all here."

"I'm sorry, Sergeant; it's possible it could be done. All of these notes will be sent to the command; ultimately it would be their decision," Mr. Smith answered.

"I see. And when will we be rotated home?"

"Home? You mean back to the United States? Boy, you really have been out of the loop."

"What do you mean?"

"I mean there is no home; the United States as you remembered it doesn't exist."

"What about all of the people? We had heard less than a few weeks ago that there were groups of survivors, that a war was waging," Brad said.

"It's complicated. Yeah, there are people there, but nothing is the way it was. Everything has broken down. Yeah, at first people went back there, but a lot of them didn't stay. Some of our crew actually fled the States. Shit, nothing is the way it was."

"Well what are we doing here, why aren't we floating off Virginia or something?"

"You know what, I'm going to try and take the time to explain things to you. It is not my job, and you are not going to like it. I can guarantee you that."

"Whatever, Mr. Smith, just tell me what the hell we are doing here."

"I was stationed at the embassy in Iraq until this shit went down. We hid in the embassy bunker for two weeks before the Marines finally got me out ... and yeah, that was back when we were still evacuating people. Trust me, Sergeant, the first time I heard it, it took me some getting used to," Mr. Smith explained.

"I have time; just tell me why we aren't going home."

"You know this was a terror attack? Or at least we are almost certain it was. Earliest reports predicted it. The classified wires warned the embassies that it was coming."

Brad nodded. "We heard the same stories, about how it started, about where they came from. We call them primals, after the name of the virus, Primalis Rabia."

"The American Continent initially held. Our government thought they had it contained. Slowly though ... borders fell. It was the worst along the southern borders. All of Central and South America poured north towards refuge, dragging the infected along with them.

"Canada was no better; yeah, they fought off the infected better, especially the more isolated parts, but eventually their governments fell. The Canadian Army moved north and inland, bringing survivors with them; they let the big cities fall. The infected ... or primal mobs moved south and flooded into New York and the Dakotas all along the land borders."

"It only took one or two primals to infect a city. Eventually states pulled away from the government defense plans. You can't blame them. In the early days, the President was using all of the federal troops to defend the Capitol. Can you imagine? Millions of primals in an open city! He sacrificed hundreds of thousands of troops on an idea. It was like the fall of Berlin. Instead of using resources to evacuate and protect the people ... he refused to give up the Capitol."

"Governors ordered their national guard troops home. States consolidated, reinforcing their own borders, using the geography to draw battle lines. Regions pooled their resources. Next the military bases began to disobey orders; instead of reinforcing the Capitol, they pledged allegiance to the state governments they were hosted in. Fort Knox was the first to switch sides. The Kentucky governor took up residence in the old gold vault. They barricaded it. Last word we had, the old home of the Armor was still holding their own."

"The planes full of troops from Afghanistan, Korea, Kuwait, Asia, and Europe would land at Fort Brag, or Benning. Once they got off the planes, they were quickly refitted and sent to the Capitol's defense. It was a meat grinder. Like sending soldiers to their deaths at Stalingrad. Except in this battle, every casualty reinforced the enemy. Eventually this stopped. Our men found out what was going on around the country and they deserted, choosing to return to their home bases or their families."

"Eventually the joint chiefs abandoned the President. They took the remaining military with them and went their separate ways. The President is presumed dead now. Or at least we think he is; it's hard to tell. There were reports he was locked away in a bunker, so he may be okay, but they lost contact with D.C. weeks ago; either way he is no longer relevant."

Brad rocked back in his chair. He couldn't believe things could fall apart so quickly.

"So then ... who is in charge?" Brad gasped.

"That's the million dollar question. There are at least three, what we would call national entities: The Midwest Alliance, the Greater Colorado Nations, and the United States of Texas. Don't get me wrong. These groups are not in competition, hell, they aren't enemies at all. They were just forced by circumstance to pull in their borders and protect their populations."

"And what about the joint chiefs?" Brad asked.

"Well, they are kind of a sub-contract house now. They still hold the banner for the United States government, but they are based out of bunkers in the Rockies. What's left of the CDC and the CIA report to them, although they're scattered. Most of the senators and members of Congress went with the joint chiefs. Still though, for the most part they are all that's collectively left of a national effort to fight this thing. They call themselves the *Coordinated National Response Team*."

Brad smiled.

"You've heard of it?"

"I have," Brad said. "Done some work for them, in fact. The Lieutenant Colonel James Cloud I told you about earlier; he said he was an officer with them."

"That name doesn't sound familiar. But for right now, they're all that is left of a federal government. They still hold most of the national assets. Aircraft, oil reserves, some of the governors will still take requests from them," Smith said.

"What about the fleet? I guess I still don't understand. Why is the fleet out here and not at home?" Brad asked.

"That's a complicated question to answer. Some say they never received solid recall orders before the fall. Maybe the joint chiefs are holding us back for another time. I haven't really been in the loop on why the fleet hasn't sailed. For now, we're building a base on the island. We send raiding and resupply teams inland to seek provisions and fuel tankers. I don't know what the long term plans are. I'm not privileged to that information."

"You don't know why we're just sitting here, or you don't want to say?" Brad asked, frustrated.

"This may surprise you, Sergeant, but I am just a low level analyst sent in here to take your statement. Everything I told you, any sailor on board could have shared with you. I don't know shit else. I was a glorified courier in Iraq; I'm nobody special," Mr. Smith said, sitting back in his chair and holding up his hands.

"I think I'd like to go back to my cell now," Brad said.

26.

Brad was led back to his room and found the space empty. The other bunks had been stripped bare and the sea bags were gone. Brad's rack was the way he had left it. The bed was still made and the green sea bag still sat next to it. He walked across the room and lay down on the mattress. "Where the hell did they go?" he said aloud.

There was a knock at the door. The handle turned and the corpsman from the day before entered the room, holding a stack of paperwork. "Afternoon, Sergeant," he said as he walked to the table and sat down.

Brad rolled to a sitting position and looked at the corpsman. "Yeah, good afternoon, I guess."

"So how are you feeling today," the corpsman asked, giving Brad a serious look.

"I'm okay, where is everyone? What's going on ... am I sick?"

"No, you're good, Sergeant. Just coming in to tell you that you have been cleared from quarantine. This is your ID badge," he said, while passing Brad a small identification card and a stuffed envelope.

"You will need to keep that badge clipped to your pocket. These are your movement papers, keep them handy," he continued. "And make sure you stick close to your assigned area, if there is anywhere you need to go, your sponsor will take you there."

Brad looked down at the white badge with a bold red border in his hand. His name and rank were on the bottom in black letters. *RESTRICTED* was across the center and *GUEST* at the top. Under the badge was a yellow envelope labeled *MOVEMENT PAPERS*.

"Movement papers?" Brad asked.

"Yeah Sergeant. You've been cleared. Go ahead and gather up all of your belongings. I need you to clear out of my medical hold. You will be moving to the island soon."

"Soon?" Brad said as he started to pack his gear.

"Depends really. There's no schedule. You just be on your toes and ready to go. They will call for you when a seat is reserved. Should be within a couple days," the corpsman said. "Someone will be along to take you down to the temporary berthing."

As the corpsman finished speaking, a new face entered the room, a jovial young man dressed in the blue navy camouflage. Smiling, he approached Brad and extended his hand. "Sergeant Thompson? I'm Winslow," he said. "I'll be taking you to your new berthing; can I help you with your gear?"

Brad shook the man's hand before turning to stuff his belongings into the sea bag. "I think I got everything ... Where are we going?"

"Just down the way, you'll like it there. More people ya know," Winslow said. "If you're ready, come on and follow me."

Brad slung the bag up over his shoulder and followed the man into the hall. He quickly noticed that the door was left unlocked and the escorts were gone. "So no more guards? You trust me now?" Brad asked as they walked.

Winslow chuckled. "Dang, Sergeant. Nahh ... That was just for infected watch; standard procedure with all the inbounds. Although we haven't had any in a long time, you know," Winslow answered.

"How long you been on this ship, Winslow?" Brad asked as he stepped through a hatch and made his way around a corner.

"Me? I been here since we sailed out of Norfolk. Shit, since the beginning I guess."

"Yeah? That's cool. So when are we going back to Norfolk?" Brad asked.

Winslow stopped walking and turned to look at Brad. "Norfolk? Did you hear we were going back?" he asked Brad, his voice suddenly turning serious.

"Ahhh yeah ... I mean ... I assumed that's where we were going," Brad bluffed.

"I don't know about that, Sergeant. Norfolk is gone, nothing there but primals. The admiral is in charge now, and I don't think he wants to go back to Norfolk. We got the island now."

"The admiral?" Brad asked.

"Yeah ... Hayes. He saved us, you know, after everything started. He pulled everything together. You got nothing to worry about, Sergeant. Hayes is real smart." Winslow looked at Brad's face as if he was searching for something, then he turned and continued to walk down the passageway.

"So nobody goes back to the States then? You don't worry about your family?" Brad questioned

"Come on, Sergeant just follow me. We'll get you settled in and you'll like it here okay," Winslow said, avoiding the question.

Nearing the end of the passage, Winslow reached down and pulled open a hatch door. "Well, here we are Sergeant, go ahead and grab yourself a rack; the head is right across from you. I have to make a quick run, then I'll be back to take you down to chow."

Brad thanked Winslow and stepped into the space. There were rows of bunks with worn mattresses, most of which appeared to be empty, so he walked toward the back of the space. He saw Brooks and Nelson sitting at a table along the back wall. The steel table was fixed to the floor and painted an ugly gray, with vinyl green bench seat cushions. Brad walked through the space and tossed his sea bag onto an empty rack as he walked toward the table.

"So what are you all thinking?" Brad said as he sat at the table.

Nelson just sat silently, shaking his head. Brooks looked up and leaned back away from the table. He strained his eyebrows as if he was searching for a thought, and then finally spoke.

"Something isn't right, Brad. I talked with a couple of the sailors, trying to dig. The fleet is just sitting static, no orders, and no movement. Just sitting at anchor and everyone seems fine with it. Like it's a blessing," Brooks said.

Brad placed his hands in front of him on the table, using his finger to scrape at the chipping paint. "I know what you're saying. I don't know whether to be frustrated or creeped out. I get that these guys have been through a lot, but shit, just sitting parked in the middle of the ocean?"

"So what do we do about it? We mess up and we might find ourselves in the brig," Brooks asked.

"You heard from Sean?"

"No, he's probably tied up in the Chief's Mess. I'll track him down later. You can count on that."

There was a clank near the front of the compartment. They heard the hatch swing open and boots slap the deck. Brad looked down the aisle and saw a smiling Winslow walking towards them. "Hey fellas, you all ready to go grab some chow? It isn't much, but it's food," he said.

Nelson was the first to his feet. He almost leapt towards Winslow. "Heck yeah buddy, just show me the way. I'm hungry enough to eat the ass end out of a buffalo!"

They followed Winslow back into the passageway and down the hall to the galley. After a short walk, they found themselves at the back of a long, slow moving line. Brad looked down the long line and shook his head. A tall sailor in front of him turned around.

"You the new guys on board?" he asked.

"Yeah, we just got here yesterday," Brad answered.

"Damn, heard you all had it rough out there."

Brad gave the sailor a puzzled look. "Yeah, I guess you could say that."

"Word travels fast on this bucket. Sorry about the wait. The ship is at close to twenty percent over-manned right now."

"Really, why is that?"

"Shit, half the fleet is dead in the water with skeleton crews doing basic maintenance. Fuel running out on most of 'em. Crews have been consolidating to the main ships. But hell, makes the work a lot easier. You know, with so many onboard. Most of us only work three days a week."

"Why don't they move everyone to the island?" Brad asked.

"Only certain personnel go to the island. Anyone responsible for keeping the ships running and floating stays onboard. You all should be leaving soon."

Brooks nudged Brad in the back to get his attention. Down the long line, he could see a number of people walking down the passage. As they got closer, he identified Sean wearing the same uniform he had been issued earlier, walking with the group. Many of the others in the party were dressed in the usual blue camouflage. A few of the men were wearing khaki uniforms.

Sean locked eyes with Brad and moved closer to him in the line. He slapped Brad briskly on the shoulder and formally asked how he was doing before he moved down to Nelson and gave the same formal greeting. Brad turned and was ready to ask Sean what was going on when he watched him shake hands with Brooks and give him a firm pat on the back. The two SEALs exchanged brief words, then Sean nodded his head and was gone.

"What the hell was that?" Brad asked, looking back at Brooks.

Before Brooks could speak, Winslow spoke up. "That's just ship politics, Sergeant; all the Chiefs and Officers making their rounds. Looks like your guy is fitting right in."

"Well, seems messed up to –," Brad began to say, then caught Brooks' disapproving glare. Brooks was slowly shaking his head side to side and gave Brad a cold stare.

"— But yeah, I know how that stuff goes. Chiefs can't be hanging out with us turds, right?" Brad said with a grin, causing Winslow to chuckle.

"Yup, even at the end of the world we still can't get along," Winslow said, laughing.

They made their way through the galley line. Unlike any mess hall Brad was accustomed to, this one was a lot smaller. The food wasn't great either. The mess attendants gave everyone the same thing without asking. The serving sizes were carefully measured and placed on the trays. Brad received a scoop of rice, a cup of black beans, and some sort of unrecognizable soup.

"Yeah, food isn't so good lately. We count on the salvage teams to supply us. So it's been a lot of beans and rice the last few weeks," Winslow explained.

They found some empty seats in the galley and sat, quickly eating their meal. Brad looked around the room and saw plenty of smiling faces. They seemed accustomed to this sort of life. You wouldn't know a war was going on outside. They just appeared to be tired from long shifts and fighting boredom.

Brad finished his food and pushed away from his tray. He watched Winslow, who was chatting with another sailor seated behind him. Suddenly there was a loud *whoomp* of an explosion; they could feel the vibration shudder across the steel floor. A claxon horn began to blast. Men calmly jumped to their feet and began pouring out of the galley.

"What the hell was that?" Brad yelled.

"Could be a lot of things. I better get you all back to your compartment. Come on, let's go," Winslow said, almost pushing them out of the galley.

27.

Winslow had quickly rushed them back down the passageway and into the compartment. He said he would be back and promised to explain what was going on later before slamming the door behind him as he left. The horn had stopped blaring but they could hear the commotion in the passageway; men running back and forth, boots on stairs, hatches opening and closing.

"This your first time on a Navy vessel, Brad?" Brooks asked.

"Yes it is. So is this kind of thing normal?" Brad answered.

"Maybe, if that was a drill, but it sure didn't sound like it; that boom sounded for real."

Brooks walked across the room and took a seat across from Brad. He reached out his hand and tossed a pack of cigarettes on Brad's lap.

"Ahh, thanks Brooks, but I don't smoke," Brad said, picking up the cigarette package.

"Yeah I get that, just open it up."

Brad lifted the lid on the cigarette package and saw it was nearly half full. He looked back at Brooks and shrugged his shoulders.

"Come on man, look a bit harder," Brooks protested.

Brad pulled back the cellophane and foil wrapper and saw a thin slip of paper wrapped around the pack. He looked up and saw Brooks was now smiling in approval. Brad removed the slip of thin paper and quickly unfolded it. It revealed a small, carefully hand-drawn map. Below the map a time was written.

"So what is this? Where did you get it?" Brad asked.

"Chief dropped it in my pocket during our brief meet and greet in the galley line," Brooks explained. "Looks like a map to the aft smoke deck; I'm thinking Chief wants to join us later."

"Why?" Nelson asked, suddenly interested in the conversation.

Brooks looked back at him. "So he can tell us what the fuck is going on. Smoking is still one of the rare acceptable things to do in private on a vessel. And one of the times you can bullshit with a chief without anyone thinking anything of it."

Brad gave Brooks a puzzled look. "You're on his team, Brooks, why haven't you been pulled out of here? I thought all of you guys stick together."

"It has definitely crossed my mind. Maybe we are intentionally being kept apart. We'll find out soon enough."

They waited quietly in their racks. Winslow had been by twice to check on them and he had blamed the loud explosion on a steam pipe bursting below decks. The expression on Brooks' face clearly showed what the SEAL's opinions were of the story. Winslow had finally left them alone at just after eight in the evening. Before he left, he said he would see them again at six a.m. to lead them to chow. Winslow also told them to stay in the compartment and try to limit their movements to the head across the hall. The guards often got jumpy at night and nobody wanted to get hurt. The men intentionally kept their plans for an evening smoke from Winslow. They wanted to leave doubts of innocence in anyone's mind in case they got caught.

Just after dark, they snuck out of the compartment and into the passageway. They left Nelson behind to play decoy and to stall any visitors that might choose to peek their heads in. If the hatch opened while they were out on their 'smoke' break, Nelson would intercept them in the compartment. His job was to distract them with random conversation to delay the discovery of the missing men.

Brad and Brooks quietly moved down the passageway following the map. Brooks had memorized the path so they wouldn't look like lost tourists. They crossed paths with a few sailors in the hall, but they walked as if they were on a mission and no one questioned them. Finally they found the exit to the aft smoke deck. Brooks stepped out first, with Brad close behind him.

The deck was large and located directly on the back of the ship. It wasn't what Brad had expected to see: no rushing water wake trailing behind them or gusts of wind – the ship rested silently in the water. Brad searched the horizon and could just make out other vessels around them. The drone of equipment and blowers made for ambient noise. The sky was filled with bright stars.

There were a couple other clusters of men, quietly chatting. It was dark and hard to make out anyone's face. Brad followed Brooks to an empty section of the rail. Brooks fished out a couple of the cigarettes. Brad used a pack of matches they had acquired and he lit up. They leaned against the rail, making casual conversation about the weather and how bad the food was. No one seemed to notice them, or even care that they were on the deck. The other sailors were preoccupied with their own group's conversations.

Brad was halfway through his cigarette and was becoming impatient. He had never been a fan of smoking, and was hoping he wouldn't have to light another one. He sensed movement at the rail next to him. Sean had finally arrived. He was alone and still wearing the tan uniform from earlier. He calmly stood against the rail and asked if he could bum a smoke.

Sean took a cigarette from Brooks and shielded the breeze as Brad used a match to light it. Sean inhaled deeply and exhaled a cloud of smoke. He casually changed his position so that he was standing just behind the other two men. To an unknowing observer, they would appear to be strangers who happen to be sharing the same space.

Sean stepped a bit closer so he was just behind their shoulders. He placed his hands in his pockets and spoke in a low voice. "Looks like you have gotten all settled in," he said.

Brad turned to speak, but Sean interrupted him. "Don't turn around ... I'm sure we're clear out here, but let's keep this very bland. If anyone notices, this was a chance encounter like in the galley line. I was told specifically not to meet with any of you until we reached the island," Sean said.

Brooks leaned out and spit over the rail. "So what's the story then? Some odd shit is definitely going on here."

"Yeah, what's with that explosion?" Brad asked.

Sean blew another puff of smoke out over the rail. "There is a lot of shit going on here. I don't have a lot of time to break everything down. What I can say is there appears to be a large portion of the crew that isn't happy with this 'new start' idea that the admiral has conjured up."

"New start? First I've heard of that," Brad said.

"Well, that is the official code name for this flotilla at sea and the island base. The admiral seems to think that the fleet is better off out here in the middle of nowhere. He plans to make a home of the island and the nuke boats; at least until the good ol' US of A gets its act together. I don't know how deep things go. I heard some rumbling that he outright refused recall orders from the Chief of Naval Ops."

Sean paused to take another drag on the cigarette before continuing.

"I'm not ready to judge the man just yet. I heard that he was warned from someone in Washington that returning would be a suicide mission. He declined the orders for the sake of the fleet. I don't know, and at this point I really don't care."

"So what does this mean for us?" Brooks asked.

"Just keep playing along, okay? Transportation has been arranged to the island tomorrow. We'll be placed on different work assignments. All of the fighter types are on salvage and recon teams. Yes Brad, I got you assigned to my group. But the rest of our people have been put on different things. Don't sweat it right now. There's already planning going on without us. There's a plan to get back stateside in the works. Brooks and I have friends here on the recon teams."

Brad nodded before speaking. "What do we do now?"

"Like I said, play along. Don't cause any problems to prevent you from going to the island and being assigned to my group."

"And the explosion?" Brooks asked.

"Some dumbass tried to steal a boat, thought he could escape to the coast. A jumpy guard dropped a grenade. A lot of stupid shit is going on. Get back to your racks and get some sleep. Act surprised when they tell you we're leaving," Sean said before he flicked the cigarette out over the rail.

After they returned to their quarters, they had a short wait before the compartment door slammed open and the bright lights were turned on. Two new faces entered the compartment, shouting about short notice for an island flight. Winslow dragged in just behind them, apologizing for the short notice while he helped them fold up their bedding and pack their limited belongings in the sea bags. Quickly, they dressed and assembled in the passageway. The two strange men had them standing against the wall, holding their bags to the side, and then they sent Winslow away. He quickly wished them good luck and disappeared down the passage.

More men started moving towards them. For the first time since they had arrived on board, Brad saw Chelsea and Tony, carrying identical sea bags and being rushed along by their own group of escorts. As the group passed them, Brad saw Sean walking in stride with another chief. Brad's group fell in behind Sean and they were rushed up to the deck. They followed a walkway around and ended up at a large helipad.

It was still dark and the morning air was cold. Brad searched the skies and saw nothing. He asked when the helicopter would be there, but was quickly asked to be quiet by his escorts. Then he noticed a pile of gear near the corner of the deck. Brad recognized the large locker that they had placed their weapons in days earlier. He saw his large rucksack and a good portion of his body armor in another pile. Brad tried to move close so that he could inspect his gear, but again he was grabbed and asked to just wait in place.

They heard the helicopter coming in; Brad recognized it as a Sea Stallion, larger than the Army's Blackhawk. It moved slowly over the water and lined up with the ship. Quickly it was on the deck, its rotor wash making communication difficult. Again they were being rushed to action. Brad felt the escort's hand grip his collar as he was somewhat shoved and guided towards the helicopter and into the open bay doors. If Sean hadn't warned him to play nice, he might have been tempted to turn and knock the pushy man on his ass.

Brad was shoved through and almost fell to the deck of the Sea Stallion. He caught himself and was guided into a seat by one of the crew. A crew chief assisted with the loading of all of their gear and slid the door shut. He gave the pilots a thumbs up, and the bird climbed up and away from the tail of the ship. Now that they were in the air, Brad could look out of the small porthole window and see the enormity of the fleet. He counted over forty large ships in the water. This was more than what he imagined a carrier strike group would normally be assigned.

Brad saw Chelsea sitting a few seats down from him. He extended out of his seat so that he could smile at her. Chelsea acknowledged him with a short wave. The helicopter was loud and they hadn't been given head phones, so verbal communication was impossible. He sat back and watched the ships fade into the distance. The helicopter leveled out and sped towards the island.

From the Sea Stallion's view, the island appeared desolate. On the approach, they flew over a teal-colored shallow lagoon before the helicopter increased elevation and covered a range of red rock formations. Brad could see the shapes of a small village in the distance, but nothing resembling an airbase.

The pilots pitched the helicopter forward and sharp to the right as it flew parallel to a dusty dirt road. The road eventually ran into and was blocked at a hastily-strewn fence. Finally the camp slowly came into view; a virtual tent city. Fixed-wing aircraft had been positioned along the sides of the dirt road, and vehicles of every type were neatly parked in a large gravel lot. The camp reminded Brad of images he had seen of the Sudan rather than a U.S. military installation.

28.

When the crew chief slid the door open, the heat hit them straight on like a blast furnace. It felt like it had to be a hundred and twenty degrees, but could have very well been hotter. Brad looked at his watch. It was barely six a.m. and the heat was already unbearable. The pilots calmly began powering down the helicopter. The hurried and rushed tempo of earlier seemed to have been left on the ship.

The crew chief removed his head gear and goggles and stepped onto the dusty road. He moved to the back of the helicopter, and Brad watched as the ramp was lowered. More men approached from out of Brad's view. They calmly walked up and started casual conversations with the helicopter's crew before one of the men walked to the open ramp and introduced himself.

"Good morning, I am Tech Sergeant Robertson of the U.S. Air Force. Please exit the helicopter from the ramp. Please grab a bag on your way out. Don't waste my time searching for your own bag; just grab something and exit. We're all headed to the same place," the man shouted.

Brad got to his feet and lined up behind the other passengers. He saw a pile of backpacks and rucksacks, along with the green sea bags. Brad spotted his large MultiCam rucksack in the pile near the large foot locker filled with weapons. He moved near the pile and grabbed the two closest bags as he followed the line out onto the gravel road.

A group of sailors had formed a work party and were taking the carried bags from the passengers before stacking them in a cart. Brad and the rest of the passengers continued walking. As Brad passed by the cart, he could see that it was harnessed to a pair of donkeys. "Where the hell have we landed?" Brad mumbled to himself.

The tech sergeant walked them across the road and to a clearing. He instructed them to line up in a formation facing west. Brad watched as their formation was joined by other passengers from helicopters that had just landed. A sailor next to Brad said they were intakes from the other ships. Brad counted close to thirty people. The donkey carts were full, and were slowly led away towards the tent city.

They were instructed to listen for their names and move to the left or the right. The tech sergeant read names from a clipboard and gave out directions. Brad heard them call Nelson, Tony, and Chelsea to the left. Soon there were only a few of them remaining in the formation. Brad finally heard his name called and was instructed to move to the right. He fell out of the formation and found a group of men gathered around a stocky Marine.

Brooks and Sean were also in the newly-formed group. The Marine introduced himself and they followed him down the dusty road. There were only six of them out of the original thirty or so that had landed. The Marine explained that they had been separated from the camp support folks and that they would be assigned to security and recon groups. First, all of them would be reunited with their weapons and gear; next, they would be assigned a housing tent.

Brad walked alongside Brooks as they stepped onto a small wooden deck positioned in front of a green tent. They were quickly briefed and split up into groups. The rest of the men were led away by escorts, while Brad found himself standing with just Brooks and Sean.

A fourth man walked out of the tent and embraced Sean in a hug, then did the same with Brooks. The man was blonde and leathered, which gave him the appearance of an old surfer dude. He looked much older than the rest of them, but he carried himself like a warrior. The man turned, looking Brad up and down.

"So who is this?" the stranger asked, pointing to Brad.

"This is Sergeant Brad Thompson. We picked him up back in the Stan, he's okay," Sean said, smiling. "Brad, this is Gunner, a prior military type, retired and gone independent contractor, but currently recalled."

"Good, well glad to have you onboard, Brad," the man said to Brad, extending his hand.

"Likewise," Brad answered, returning the handshake. "So what kind of contractor were you?"

"Mostly security stuff, embassy escorts, some transportation shit. Got stuck in Qatar on my last job. Made my way down here," Gunner said.

"And what exactly is this here?" Brad asked.

Gunner stopped and looked back at Sean. Sean just grinned and shrugged his shoulders. "You know what? You guys make your way to the carts and grab up your gear before it disappears on you. We are in tent six at the end of this row. Charlie Group is our designation. Charlie works and sleeps out of tent six. Go get settled in and then I'll show you around. We're off the rotation for a day or two so we have some time to settle in."

Brad followed Sean and Brooks toward the now nearly empty cart. He found his rucksack on the ground along with the issued sea bag from the ship. His bag had obviously been gone through, but it was hard to tell what was missing. Sean lowered the locker from the cart and opened the lock. Their weapons and ammunition were still there. For now, they reclaimed only their sidearms, and left the rest in the locker.

Brad grabbed Brooks' rucksack along with his own, while Brooks hoisted the heavy locker onto his shoulder. Together they followed Sean towards tent six. The tents' openings were lined up with the road and were stacked west towards the fence. Each tent had a small deck in front and a wooden stake giving it a designation. Tent six was as nondescript as the rest of them. Sean stepped forward and pulled back the flap covering the entrance.

The sides of the tent had been rolled up to allow for air flow. Normally, in the best of times, air conditioning units would be set up to make the tents livable. In this camp, air conditioners were not an option. The tents were old; the floors were made up of scrap planks and lumber material. Instead of the bunks, there were rows of issue cots lined up along one wall. No lockers or even foot lockers were present. This was Spartan living at its finest.

Sean headed toward a section of empty cots. Most of them had gear piled on top, and a few contained sleeping men. Brad dropped his heavy rucksack on an empty cot and tossed Brooks' rucksack on another. Sean selected an empty cot across from them. They opened their rucksacks and took inventory of their gear before Brooks opened the locker and distributed their weapons. They made note to try and get the remaining rifles to the Marines.

Gunner walked through the tent's opening and jokingly complimented them on their cot selection. Sean talked to him about the Marines' weapons and Gunner said he would make sure they got sent to the support side. After getting more instructions on the rules of the tent, as well as the location of the latrines and mess tents, Gunner asked them to finish what they were doing and follow him back outside.

Brad put on his holster and checked the magazines for his M4. Quickly he closed the straps on his rucksack and left it on top of his cot, then got to his feet and joined the rest of them on the deck. Gunner asked them to follow him down a narrow, roughly-built boardwalk as he talked to them. While they walked, Brad could see that the camp was awake and a bustle of activity was going on near the airfield.

"Place doesn't look like much," Gunner said as he walked. "But trust me, this is a fully functioning camp. We are trying to become self-sufficient. We've captured some large fuel tankers from the Gulf, but most of the fuel goes to the fleet and the few aircraft we still have operational."

They approached a fork in the boardwalk at the end of the row of tents. The path branched off with one leg moving toward the gate and the other off toward the makeshift airfield. Gunner stepped off the trail here and they followed him up an incline of rocks. Finally they were on a small outcrop that overlooked the camp. Brad could see that the main fence still continued around the rocks, although in some places it was no more than strands of barbed wire. But they were still entirely contained.

Sean looked down at the tent city., "How many boots on ground?"

"Close to five grand, not counting those in the fleet. Maybe another five or so in the village. Not sure about those numbers, we haven't taken time to do a good count." Gunner answered.

"The village?" Brooks asked.

"Yeah, there's a small village on the shore. Farm people and fisherman. Good folks, a lot of them are already employed by us. They provide a lot of food to the camp."

Gunner stepped off and climbed farther up the hill until he found a spot with large flat rocks. He leaned back against one and fished a cigarette from his pocket. He offered one to the rest of them but they declined.

"So what's the outlook here, Gunner?" Sean asked.

"Not good, Brother. I don't see how things here can end well. The admiral is pushing for a new start. He sent us out on raids to the main land, salvaging goods and supplies. We have had some luck raiding major ports, but the planes are too small to bring back anything substantial."

"You finding any survivors out there?" Sean asked.

"Some, but not many. The ones we do see run or hide from us. There are a lot of bandits on the mainland. Lately we've been looking for ghost ships. The fleet will grab them on radar and we'll take them down. If they have goods worth taking, we bring them back and we take in the crews if they're healthy. We've only had a couple of radar contacts in the last few weeks though."

Brad tossed a rock and finally spoke up. "Eventually supplies will run out and this is a desert island. How do they plan to feed everyone when the fuel dries up?"

"Exactly. This has become a heated discussion. At first the admiral said this was just a rest stop while we waited to see how things played out at home. Now he's making long term plans. Yes this place is secure, I give him that. But people don't like it here and the ones that try to escape are dealt with harshly."

"What happens to them?" Brad asked.

"Let me just say we don't have a prison here. They say they take them back to the fleet. But I have heard rumors they are ditched at sea. No room for troublemakers out here."

"Alright, so let's get down to it. What is our exit strategy, Gunner? I've known you long enough to know this isn't your home," Sean said, giving Gunner a serious stare.

"I already know you spoke to Master Chief Swan on board the Barry. He's the one who called ahead and made sure you got assigned to Charlie Group. Not like that was a lot of trouble," Gunner smiled. "He also told me your sergeant here can be trusted, so I hope that pans out for us."

"Brad is one of us, don't worry about him. So what's the plan?" Sean asked again.

"Charlie Group is mainly responsible for heavy inland recons. In two days, we're supposed to be hitting Yemen main. A city on the coast. They usually bring us in and drop us off by CH-53. We set up security and gather salvaged supplies in large cargo nets. If we locate any large holds we tag and mark them with a GPS for later recovery. A few hours later, the 53s come back, we sling-load the cargo, and get out of Dodge."

"Sounds like a lot of work, but continue," Sean said.

"Well, day after tomorrow we're going to change things up. As soon as we're dropped, we're going to beeline for the airport. One of the kids in Bravo Group fought his way through there before being plucked from the embassy. He thinks they still have some heavy lift fixed-wings on the ground."

"Not a lot to go on, is it?" Brooks said.

"No, it's not. Pilots have flown over the airport in the past few weeks. They have confirmed aircraft on the ground, but who knows if we can get them in the air."

"What's the city look like?" Brooks asked.

"One hundred percent fucking infested. But hey! Only the dead live forever ..." Gunner laughed. "Are we all on board with this or what?"

Brad stood and took a step towards Gunner. "Gunner, I can fully commit to your plan, but we came with other people. We need to get them out also. Or at least offer them the opportunity."

"Yeah, I know. Master Chief told me you all came with more troops." Gunner sighed before continuing. "Here's the thing. I've done a bit of ground work and requested some mechanics for our next raid. Said we might be looking for operational generators and shit like that. It's going to be tough to explain why I need the three greenest techs on the camp, but that gets me your Marines. The pilots and two civilians are another problem; I don't see how I can pull them in without raising red flags."

"Just see what you can do, I understand we can't save everyone," Sean said.

"Save everyone? Are you shitting me, Sean? Do you know what's waiting for us back home? This place is a paradise compared to what's back there. If anything, we're all headed to a quick death," Gunner said.

He looked Sean in the eyes. "I was stateside when this shit started. I got stuck doing State Department escorts. Running high level-types home from the embassies. Most of the big stuff was busy, we took private jets."

"You were back home? What's it like?" Brad asked.

"Last time I was there I was taking a family back from Jordan. We landed at Andrews; Reagan had already been overrun. When we flew over we could see that the city was a burning mess; they had road blocks everywhere, but most of them were down. Military was scattered, no command, and no control. The family begged me to take them back to Jordan. But that wasn't in the works."

"What happened to them?"

"They were taken away by State Department vehicles," Gunner said, shaking his head. He reached into his pocket for another cigarette. "The jet was refueled and rushed me back to Qatar for another pickup. City was dark when we got there; airport was empty. We damn near crash landed. Runway lights were all off and we clipped a utility vehicle on the ground.

"My team and I left the pilots on the ground. They were going to try and secure transportation. We grabbed a vehicle and headed to the embassy over land. It was poor decision-making on my part. We only made it two blocks. We fought our way to an apartment roof and held up for three days. Never heard from the pilots again. On the fourth day, a Chinook picked up my distress beacon and got us out of there. We sat at the embassy for two more days before the admiral finally pulled us out.

"If you are planning to go back to the States because you think it's better than this ... think again. We all have our reasons for going back. Safety won't be one of them."

Sean slapped Gunner on the back. "Understood, Gunner; that just came out wrong. I appreciate the plans you have laid out. Let me track down my Marines. We'll be ready to roll with you when we get the go."

"Brief them on the raid mission only, don't say shit else. No one outside of us knows the real intentions of tomorrow's mission. We'll let them make that choice on the ground. After the CH-53 drops us in the city, we'll wire up a perimeter. If they decide to not go back with us, the birds will be back to take them home ... Long after we are gone," Gunner said with a grin.

"Don't worry, Gunner; they'll want to go with us. We've been through a lot," Brad said.

29.

The trio found the Marines late that night, gathered outside of the chow tents. Chelsea said her group leader had already informed them about the raid. Sean didn't elaborate on the mission or why they were selected to join Charlie Group, just that he wanted experienced Marines on his raid, people that he could trust, and not a bunch of broke ass sailors with no boots-on-ground time. The Marines were excited to be back working with Sean again.

Sean gave them a detailed packing list for the mission and left them. Gunner had warned him again about spending a lot of time with people outside of the group. The camp's cohesiveness had broken down, and rumors spread fast. They didn't want anyone getting suspicions about the real intentions of the raid. The trio went back to tent six and did their own pre-combat checks and inspected their equipment.

Brad found that most of his gear was still present. After a good washing, he reverted back to his Army issue MultiCam uniform and stuffed the Navy crap back into his sea bag. He did keep the boots though; his old ones had a lot of miles on them and were starting to fall apart. The only things he noticed missing were his scout binoculars and most of his spare magazines for the M4.

Sean was pissed when he discovered the satellite phone was gone along with the batteries. Even though it had been useless to them for a while, they had gone through a lot of trouble to get it, and he wasn't happy to see it missing. Sean and Brooks decided to stay in their familiar Navy uniforms, not because they liked them, but because the civilian gear they had been wearing was a mess and was ripping at the seams.

Gunner took them to the supply building, one of the few hardened structures on the camp. Each of the trio were issued a new fighting knife, which Brad thought was of far less quality than the karambit he already carried. He figured he would pass the new one off to a Marine.

They were also given a small pry bar and a tactical tomahawk, along with a bundle of batteries, more spare magazines, and some new gloves. Each of them was given a Kevlar shirt which the supply petty officer called a bite shirt. He explained the shirt was originally designed when working with sharpened sheet metal on aircraft, but had also proven useful in close combat with primals.

Gunner explained to them that there were not many recon members in the camp and, because of the shortage of gun fighters, they had been stuck doing most of the heavy lifting. This niche status earned them a nice cache of weapons and equipment. The recon groups received better food at chow and they had more freedom of movement on the island.

Another benefit of being on a recon team was that you did not have to participate in the daily camp duties. No working in the mess hall, filling sand bags, or burning shit. Still though, one or two days a week you were expected to go into the infected cities and face off against the primals. When the mission was over, a twenty-four hour quarantine would be waiting for you.

The admiral had tried to give his war fighters the best to keep them happy. The security of the camp was held together by the compliance of the recon groups. One thing the admiral didn't understand was that the same thing that gave them the courage to run down primals, was also what burned at them to return home to their country and their families, even if it meant certain death.

Morning came hot and fast to the island. Brad woke early, since it was impossible to sleep under the intensity of the sun. He rose from his cot and followed the others to the showers and latrine. He had briefly met the members of Charlie Group the previous night. It had been late though, and there were no lights in the tent, so introductions were brief.

Charlie Group was made up almost entirely of combat arms soldiers, sailors and Marines. There were seven of them, including Gunner. Most of them had worked together for weeks, since the founding of the island camp. Gunner had joined the group early, and as the senior member had become their leader. He was responsible for the recruiting and training of the members as well as the planning of missions. The rest of Charlie Group referred to Gunner as 'The Godfather', which somehow had broken down to just 'Pops'.

The only female in the group and exclusive non-combat arms member was Lieutenant Kelli Davis. She had been a competitive shooting champion in high school, and ranked top junior pistol shot in her state for three years. It was said her skills with a rifle were even better. She was raised a country girl, hard as nails, and could hunt and track with the best of them.

Gunner sent a request through the chain of command for Kelli to join Charlie Group. They resisted at first, but Gunner was a hell of a salesman and eventually they came around. He was in need of a sniper and she would fit the position. The guys in charge signed off on the request, but that's not why he'd recruited her. She was a naval aviator and had trained on large cargo aircraft. Charlie Group had needed a pilot, and they got one.

The Villegas brothers were from Southern California. Dark, lean, and mean Marine Corps reservists doing a nine-month tour in Kuwait during the fall, they had managed to escape deep into the desert during the first days. They had survived for weeks on their own before being spotted by a low-flying observation plane. Now they were designated rifleman in Charlie Group. Quiet, tough, and reliable was how they were described.

The last three members of Charlie Group were plucked from the top of a Bradley fighting vehicle in the dunes of Saudi Arabia. Sergeant Hahn, Corporal Parker, and Specialist Theo had been cavalry scouts assigned to an armored cavalry regiment. The scouts had fought a rolling retreat all the way from central Iraq. Tip of the spear. Lead vehicles in a massive convoy which had been rolling south towards the southern border. During an intense late night engagement, a fuel vehicle had bogged down on a bridge. They had pulled into a defensive perimeter and called the recovery vehicles forward, fighting wave after wave as the combat engineers attempted to clear the route. A lot of people and ammunition were lost in the failed effort. The more the soldiers fought, the more primals were attracted in. Vehicle crews ran out of ammunition and a means to fight back, then their fuel tanks had run dry. In the early morning hours, crews on the south side of the bridge were ordered by the officer in charge to continue the withdrawal and move towards the Saudi border, while vehicles to the north would search for a new route. Vehicles broke out of the defensive formations and scrambled to escape the primal mobs. Hahn's Bradley was down to a driver and gunner; he had lost all of his dismounts early in the battle. Hahn commanded his vehicle south, fighting his way through the desert. In the chaos, they became separated from the rest. Radios were stormed with panicked traffic. Without the support of the convoy, their vehicle ran out of fuel and they became stranded and alone, lost in the Saudi desert. Sergeant Hahn and his men were rescued two days later.

The back portion of tent six contained a makeshift ready room: a small table surrounded by cobbled-together benches. When Brad filed into the tent, he found most of Charlie Group already assembled in the briefing area. He was surprised to see Chelsea, Nelson, and Craig occupying a bench near the back of the space. Brooks had followed in behind Brad, and stood next to a pole that supported the weight of the tent.

Sean and Gunner entered the room through a side door, causing everyone to suddenly cease conversations and take their seats. Gunner took a seat near the table and Sean found a seat near him. Even though they all shared a common goal in getting back to the States, Gunner had decided early on that he would keep everyone in the dark until they reached the drop zone. Operational security had to be tight for everything to succeed.

Gunner pulled a sheet off the table, uncovering a map underneath. "Hope everyone is rested up, we have a big op planned for tomorrow. I gather everyone has met the new members of Charlie Group. These guys have a lot of experience on the ground with screamers; experience we can use. Also, tomorrow's mission will be augmented with the Marines.

"They are mechanics and electricians. We are tasked with trying to locate and recover working generators. The wrench turners will help, so let's not get them killed right off."

Hahn raised his hand and gave Gunner a cold stare, "Excuse me Gunner, but how in the hell are we supposed to kill screamers while we are babysitting these kids?"

"Fair enough question, Hahn. We'll split into two, six-man teams for tomorrow. You six will run the same as always, as the Alpha element. Chief Rogers will take his people and the techs as Bravo element. I'll stay in command."

Gunner pointed to a spot on the map overlay. "We're going to drop in on the roof of this large office structure. From there, we'll run a standard perimeter and observation post, before we branch out on our search recons. We'll have approximately one hundred and eighty minutes on the ground. Pickup will be on the same rooftop."

Hahn again raised his hand. "Pops, what's the alternate rally and pickup point in case things go bad?"

"So glad you asked that, Sergeant Hahn," Gunner said, as he used his grease marker to circle a section on the far corner of the map. "This is plan B, it's an airport. If the shit hits the fan, we will roll hard to the alternate pickup point."

"Pops, that's damn near five clicks through open terrain! One hell of a hump if we're in active retreat," Hahn said.

"True story; thank you for recognizing the risk for us. I want all of you to memorize this map and possible routes to plan B. Sergeant Hahn makes a good point about the dangers, so let's take double ammo and rations tomorrow just in case," Gunner said to the moans of the others.

"Damn Pops, double ammo and rations? That's a lot of gear to hump," the elder Villegas, Daniel, protested.

The younger Villegas, Joey, let out a deep laugh, "Shoot, big brother, if it's too much for your old ass, I'll carry your shit for you."

"Yo shut up man, I'll carry my own shit!" Daniel snapped back.

"Okay, okay, that's enough, get your stuff together. Everyone on the road tomorrow at zero three. That is all." Gunner said.

The room fell to silence as Gunner and Sean walked out of the tent. The rest of the members gathered around the table, taking notes and drawing sketches of the objective. Brad decided to avoid the crowd and went outside to grab some fresh air. He went beyond the tents and walked the road toward the large camp.

Sensing he was being followed, he turned back and saw Chelsea coming up behind him. He stopped to wait up for her. "Can I join you, Sergeant Thompson?" she asked with humor in her voice.

"You may, Corporal Swanson," he answered as they continued to walk the road.

"So Brad, what the hell are we doing here? Do you know what is going on?" Chelsea asked.

Brad stopped and looked behind him before answering her. "Chelsea, just relax and go with things. We just got here. You'll get adjusted to the routine."

"I don't care; I didn't sign up to be making garbage runs into cities. This isn't my job. I just want to get home. I don't want to adjust, Brad."

"Everyone wants to get home, but for now this is the hand we have been dealt. Get your people together. Inspect their gear and make sure they are ready for tomorrow's mission."

"I'm not interested in the mission, can't they find someone else?"

"What did you tell me back on the tower? You said don't quit. So suck it up, Marine. I don't want to hear this bullshit out of you again. Do you understand?" Brad said, his frustration growing. Not only with her attitude, but because he couldn't tell her the true objectives of the mission.

"Yes Sergeant! Understood," Chelsea said before she turned to walk away, but not before Brad saw the hurt in her expression.

30.

The Sea Stallion's blades were already turning at high speed. The roar of the engines and the wash of dust made communication impossible. Gunner was just outside the radius of the large rotor blades, speaking to the helicopter's crew chief. Then he ran back to the edge of the road where the rest of Charlie Group had assembled, and pulled Sergeant Hahn and Sean off to the side.

Everyone was standing nervously over their gear of overstuffed rucksacks and long rifles, waiting for instructions. Each of them was dressed in their newly-acquired bite shirts under their heavy body armor. Brad and the other three soldiers were in MultiCam while the rest wore the tan, Navy issue uniforms. Brad looked to Chelsea to try and get her attention; she saw his stare and looked away.

Sean and Hahn ran to the group, yelling for them to move out. Brad grabbed his heavy rucksack and looped the straps over his shoulders. He joined in line behind the rest of Charlie Group running toward the loading ramp of the aircraft. He followed until the line quickly stopped, then dropped into a seat on the port side. When everyone was onboard and set, Gunner flashed a thumbs up to the crew chief.

Slowly the CH-53 rose into the still dark, early morning sky. The ramp remained down and they could see the dim outlines of the darkened camp as they flew away back out over the Arabian Sea and towards the Gulf of Aden. Quickly they were up and at cruising speed; the two hundred mile trip to the main land would take them just over an hour. The sun was starting to break the horizon and the sky glowed in response.

Brad tried to relax. He went over the checklists in his head. He didn't have to worry about forgetting anything; everything he owned was in his pack or on his person. He was carrying food and water for six days, which might seem like a lot, but not for continuous operations. Lately he had trained himself to survive on as little as one meal a day. One high calorie meal a day had done little to prevent the weight loss he had experienced in the last month.

He had two hundred and ten rounds of 5.56 ammo strapped to his vest and another hundred and forty rounds in his pack. He carried seventy-five rounds of 9mm ammo, not counting the fifteen rounds loaded into his Sigma pistol. The tomahawk was strapped to his hip, his fighting knife on the left breast of his armor. Brad had reluctantly discarded his helmet in exchange for a lightweight boonie cap. He had two changes of uniform and a light poncho liner in a bivy sack. Altogether, his kit was over eighty-five pounds.

The helicopter flared and changed altitude as they approached the coast line. The CH-53 cut right to approach the city in a slow, sweeping arc, out and away from their true objective. Just as in normal combat operations, the idea was to deceive the enemy of their true landing point. The helicopter neared the edge of the city and several times made false insertions.

The crew chief gave a five minute warning and everyone gripped onto their rucksacks and weapons. The Sea Stallion made another dry landing nearly two blocks from the target building before it leapfrogged up and sped to the actual drop site. The bird lowered and hovered just over the building as the crew chief yelled for them to get out. Quickly they grabbed their gear and poured out of the helicopter. The Sea Stallion crew members grabbed web and sling load materials and dumped it onto the deck just as the throttles went up and the helicopter roared away.

Brad watched as it made more false insertions and slowed its speed to lure any hunting primals away from the target building. Charlie Group cleared the area and made a full circle perimeter along the inside of the roof. They had formed a basic perimeter with the Alpha element taking responsibility of covering the two rooftop entrances. Then they dropped and became silent, listening for any movement, and smelling the air for signs of the primals.

Brad sat uncomfortably; he had unwisely chosen a position amongst broken stone and debris. The sun was now in full force and he could feel the sweltering heat and the sweat rolling down his back. The building they had chosen was three stories high. The roof was constructed of concrete but mainly held together by asphalt. The edges of the roof were skirted by a three-foot wall. Small vents, chimneys, and two roof access structures were almost randomly placed.

Brad quickly made a visual check of the rest of the Bravo element. Sean was in the middle of the hasty perimeter kneeling next to Hahn and Gunner. Chelsea and the other techs were in a broken line along the east end of the roof. Brooks had taken up a crouched position near the south wall where he could observe both roof access structures.

After waiting over ten minutes in silence, Gunner stood and called everyone to his position near the center of the roof. Brad got to his feet in the middle of the debris and looked around to make sure everyone had received the message. Brad reached for his rucksack that he had dropped near him just after exiting the helicopter. As he grabbed the top handle and went to lift the bag, he felt a sagging in his knees and heard the creaking sound of splitting wood. He quickly released the handle and stood motionless. For an instance he had felt a sensation of dropping. He relaxed and took a deep breath as he slowly took a step forward.

Just as he leaned forward the roof gave out from underneath him. He dropped fast as if a trap door had opened. He slipped feet first with no time to outstretch his arms. He slapped his face on a beam as he fell through layers of rotted wood and asphalt. He consciously fought to hold on to his rifle as he slapped into, then through, a large pile of debris. He felt as if he was lying on piles of rotten bodies and skeletons. A hot white flash of pain rushed through his body.

He couldn't see. The quick movement from the bright outdoors to the dark interior of the building had blinded him. He quickly checked every inch of his body for injuries. He felt okay, except for the stinging burn on his face and the taste of blood on his lips. He stretched out his arms and felt the cushioned mess around him. Brad went to straighten his legs and felt the searing pain in his thigh. Apprehensively he dropped his arm and felt a large wooden splinter piercing through the top of his leg. He had apparently fallen into a junk room loaded with piles of broken furniture and masses of garbage bags filled with refuse.

Brad could see light from the hole he had fallen though, a narrow break in the roof maybe ten to twelve feet above him. He tried to stand but found himself tangled in the mass of broken furniture and garbage bags. The pain was unbearable, and made putting weight on his right leg impossible. He heard a voice call his name from above. They were obviously trying to stay away from the break in the roof. He shouted back a quick reply.

Brad again tried to untangle himself from the debris when he heard the first moan. *'Oh shit,'* he said to himself as he lay there, silently listening. He concentrated on trying to find the source of the noise. There was a skirmish of activity behind him and the noise sounded muted, possibly through a wall. Brad closed his eyes and slowly opened them again, trying to let the light from the hole in the ceiling bleed into the room.

He began to make out the far wall, maybe ten feet away. He could see garbage and debris all around him; it was piled thick to the ceiling and pressed against a battered and destroyed door. *'Oh no,'* he thought again as he realized where he had fallen. He was positioned in the middle of a makeshift barricade. Brad twisted hard in the garbage and was able to make out a larger portion of the room opening up into the darkness.

'Now,' the question he asked himself. *'Are there primals in the room? Or are they all on the other side of the barricade?'* Another moan, coming from deep within the dark corners of the room, answered his question. The moan was joined by more screams from the other side of the door. Brad saw a shadow in the light above; he strained his eyes to see Brooks lying flat looking, into the hole.

"You okay down there?" Brooks yelled.

"Leg is dicked up, but I'll live, if that's what you are asking. I'm also not alone, if you were curious."

"Yeah I can hear the bastards, how many?"

"Hell, I don't know," Brad said, shouting over a building chorus of screams and moans. "Sounds like a swarm. I have at least one of them in the room with me; the rest are on the other side of a door."

"What did you fall in, buddy? You're in a rat's nest of shit down there; can you crawl out?"

Brad bent his body and strained his arms, trying to get a handle onto something solid. He reached a long, broken board and was able to get a few fingers around it. He began to pull hard to straighten himself; getting his other arm around the board, he pulled with all of his strength. Just as he finished pulling himself to a painful kneeling position, there was a crash into the pile. A primal had hit it at a full on run. It was snarling and thrashing at the barricade, trying to get at Brad.

Brad was now in complete panic mode, scrambling to get out of reach of the creature, ignoring the pain, and fighting off the shock. With no room to maneuver the M4, he pulled his M9 and tried to get a good angle. Holding the pistol with a bent arm, he fired at the frenzied creature which was moving fast and jumping around the pile. Brad fired again, unsure if he hit it. He fired a third time and saw a portion of the creature's jaw explode, but it continued to come at him, attacking the barricade from different directions. Brad pressed hard against the obstacles behind him, using his good leg to press back and create a dead space. He brought up the pistol, took careful aim, and finally put down the primal.

The same gunshots that had killed his immediate threat also sounded the dinner bell for the crazies on the other side of the door. Brad forced his way through the pile, crawling and dragging himself toward the creature he had just killed to get to the inside of the room and out of the barricade. As he crawled, he looked back toward the door and saw the first of many hands grab at the battered wooden door.

"Talk to me down there, I can't see shit from up here!" Brooks yelled.

Brad finally freed himself from the barricade and out of the cluster of garbage. He slipped, rolled to the hard floor, and then rolled back further, falling flat on his back onto a carpet. He looked around and saw more loose refuse and garbage. Brad struggled at his armor and finally located his flashlight. He quickly panned it around the void, relieved to find he was alone. The single primal must have occupied this hide out. It had probably been wounded somehow and turned here alone, or was abandoned here. Either way, it was not his problem.

"I'm clear, but there are a lot of them trying to get in," Brad yelled up to Brooks.

Brad took a look at his leg; a large, broken piece of wood had entered the right side of his thigh, piercing through the top of his leg. It came clean through the top and there was no bleeding, so he hoped it missed the artery. There was no time for self-surgery, so he wrapped and stabilized the splinter as best he could with dressings made from his gear. Another pounding and a sound of ripping wood woke his thoughts again.

Brad holstered the M9 and swung his suppressed M4 back into action. He watched the break in the door as creatures poured out. The barricade looked like hell, but it seemed to do the job. Everything that poured into it was quickly bogged down in the piles of broken furniture and garbage. At least five of them had breached the door and were piled into the mess now.

Brad heard the blast of a twelve gauge shotgun come from above, then another crash and the sporadic sounds of suppressed small arms fire.

"Hold on buddy, Alpha element is on its way down. They just breached the door," Brooks shouted.

"No, come on man, I can't get out through that door. It's blocked solid by the barricade," Brad shouted back over the roaring of the primals.

"Don't worry about it, just keep yourself safe," Brooks yelled.

Brad raised the suppressed rifle to his shoulder and took an aimed shot. He struck one of the tangled creatures square in the top of the head. Slowly, Brad used his hands to right himself and to move farther back into the room against a far wall. He propped himself up and raised his rifle, killing another primal that was burrowing through the barricade. Brooks kept calling down, telling him to hold tight. Alpha was in the hallway and would be on him shortly.

There was a muffled explosion. Brad saw sparks from outside the destroyed door. The rest of the door was yanked back and off of its hinges. He heard the men outside shouting instructions, and a light shone into the pile. The last three primals were quickly put down. Brad tried to stand; he struggled but made it to his feet. He looked into the blinding light.

"You okay in there, bro?" he heard the elder Villegas call out to him.

"I'm good, but I can't get out that way."

"Okay bro, get away from that wall. We fixing to make a new door," Daniel answered.

The men left their position outside of the door. Brad heard more gunfire and the shouting of soldiers. Soon there was a pounding at the wall, followed by a muffled yell warning him to get away. There was a loud yell down the hall of *"Fire in the hole"* just as the room exploded and a sharp crack cut Brad's hearing. He couldn't see anything; the room was a cloud of dust and debris, and his ears were ringing. Brad struggled again to stand as the men rushed the room and grabbed him.

Quickly they dragged him through the breached wall. Two men carried Brad, two more cleared the way out front, and another two took up the rear. They passed through a cluttered apartment and into a trashed hallway. They moved quickly up and over dead primals. They found the stairway, turned the corner, and the lead men stopped to cover the stairs that led down while the men carrying Brad moved him back up to the roof. Brad was moved several feet from the door just as everyone came onto the roof and the door was secured.

Brad was carefully placed on his back near the wall's skirt. Quickly, Brooks cut Brad's uniform away from the wound. He reached in his aid bag; finding what he was looking for, he went to stick Brad. "No ... Don't. There's no casualty evacuation coming for me, I have to stay sharp," Brad said.

Brooks gave Brad a worried look and shook his head, "I don't think you have a choice, Brad. I can't fix this. Unless you go back on the return chopper, you won't get any treatment," Brooks said.

Chelsea came forward and kneeled near Brad. "Let him give you the morphine. The helicopter will be back and they can treat you. We can secure the roof until then," she said.

Brad looked up at Sean. "Tell them."

Gunner stepped forward. He told them about the egress plan; the move to the airport. How they had all needed to be gone when the CH-53 returned for the pickup. Yes, there was an option to stay behind and return on the bird, but he hoped they would choose to attempt the airfield. They needed to make a decision, and quick.

"Brooks, my leg isn't broken. Pull this shit out and wrap it tight. I'll make it with you guys or die trying," Brad said. "You can leave my gear, I don't care, but I'm not going back."

Brooks looked to Gunner and Sean for an answer. "Get started on the ropes to rappel down. Secure us a vehicle on the ground. I didn't feel like walking anyhow. We can still do this. Brooks, get him patched up; we'll come for you when it's time to move out," Gunner said.

The men jumped to their feet, moving back to the wall and preparing ropes. Sean came to Brad's side. "Brooks is going to work with you; don't worry, we will get you out of here, Brad. Chelsea, stay and help Brooks, I'm going with your guys to grab us some wheels."

Brooks put the morphine injector back in his pack and pulled out a Fentanyl lollipop. "Here, put this in your mouth. I'll pull that out of your leg but I'm not doing it to you cold."

Brad nodded and opened his mouth as Brooks put the medicated stick on his tongue and swabbed the inside of Brad's mouth. Soon Brad began to feel his pain numb. Brooks ordered Chelsea to try and hold Brad down as best she could while he worked on his leg. Brooks rolled Brad onto his stomach and Chelsea knelt across Brad's right hip. Brad could feel the weight and he felt Brooks pull on his right knee to straighten his leg.

There was a searing pain as Brooks tugged and pulled the large splinter out. "Good news! Looks like it just went through your quad. Surprisingly looks pretty clean," Brooks said as he doused the wound with water and a peroxide solution. Then he quickly covered both sides of the wound with quick-clot bandages and tightly wrapped it with clean dressings. When he was finished, he pulled as much of the uniform pants back over the wound as possible and then wrapped it again with a small roll of electrical tape.

"This is temporary, Brad. I'm going to have to open it up and clean it as soon as possible. I need you to start taking these right away," Brooks said, handing Brad a small bottle of antibiotics. "Keep that lollipop handy; you're going to be in a lot of pain. I still have the morphine stick if you want it later," Brooks finished.

"I'm good; just let me catch my breath. I'll be ready to go when they give the word," Brad said, sweating and grimacing in pain.

They carried Brad closer to the building's wall while they lowered their gear below. Brooks helped Chelsea onto the ropes and she slowly rappelled herself to the ground. Next, Brooks positioned Brad into an under-the-shoulder harness, strapped him in, and lowered him down. Brad landed with his good leg and dropped onto a sunbaked sidewalk next to the building. Brooks dropped beside him and undid the harness.

The city was empty and void of movement. The sidewalk and road were empty except for the strewn garbage piled at the corners of the streets. Brad leaned against the hot wall, shielding his eyes from the sun. He fished through his pockets and found his tinted goggles – he must have lost his glasses in the fall. Brad put them on to shield his eyes from the bright sun. He could see members of the Alpha element positioned down both sides of the street. Farther down, he could see more men gathered around an abandoned vehicle. It looked like a Volkswagen van from the front. There was a small four-door cab in the front, with a small pickup truck-type bed in the back.

They had pushed the van out and away from the curb. The Marines had the hood open and were leaning over the engine compartment. Brad watched as Sean jumped in the cab and barked instructions. The Marines got behind the vehicle and pushed it. Sean popped the clutch, the vehicle stuttered and coughed, then backfired loudly before dying. The Marines ran back to the vehicle and tried again.

The Alpha element was nervously scanning the surroundings, knowing the noise would attract the screamers. Again the van stuttered, but this time it coughed to life. Sean eased in the clutch and revved the engine until he achieved an idle. Sean slowly nursed the van down the narrow street on badly bald tires, while the Marines followed behind him at a jog to keep up. The van pulled up near Brad and rested against the curb.

Sean shouted instructions from the window. Everyone gathered their gear and threw it into the back of the van. They lifted Brad and placed him in the bed atop all of the gear. Brad crawled so that his back was against the cab of the van and positioned his rifle so that he could cover his side of the vehicle. They dropped the tailgate on the truck and piled in, grabbing onto the sides while the remaining four jumped in the cab. There were thirteen of them packed into a vehicle made for half of that.

Brad's pain had greatly subsided, so he took the lollipop from his mouth and placed it into his breast pocket for safe keeping. He could still feel the pressure and tightness in his leg even though the pain had been numbed. He tried straightening and bending his leg in the confined space, and was able to do it with minimal discomfort. He could feel the tightening of the tissue and was careful not to put too much pressure on the wound.

Brad watched Specialist Theo load his M203 grenade launcher with a 40-millimeter grenade. He aimed high into the sky and popped the round out and into the distance. There was a thump from the 203 as it landed some three hundred meters away before the sharp explosion. Theo loaded another round and again aimed out and over a neighboring building. Another thump was followed by a distant blast. "What the hell is he shooting at?" Brad asked.

Corporal Parker looked at Brad as the van began to drive up the street toward the airport. "He's not shooting at anything, Sergeant. We found out a while ago that the forty mike-mikes are more useful at drawing the primals away then they are at fighting them. So whenever we need to make a move in Indian country, we lob a couple off in the distance to get them headed in the wrong direction."

"We use flares," Brad joked.

"What the fuck? Y'all is crazy, we don't mess with them at night," Parker answered.

The van's engine smoothed out as it warmed up and picked up speed. Sean guided it down the middle of the street, only slowing to avoid vehicles or obstacles on the road. They made their way through the heaviest parts of the city, only spotting an occasional primal in the distance. The CH-53 false insertions combined with the M203 distraction must have been successful in leading them away.

Charlie Group quickly reached the outer perimeter of the airport. Instead of driving around and looking for an entrance, Sean pulled up alongside a high chain link fence. A number of men jumped from the vehicle and began quickly cutting a gap in the fence. They pulled a section back, allowing the van to ease through. The men hastily repaired the gap before re-boarding the van. Sean gunned the van and headed toward the runway.

The runway was scattered with small aircraft. Brad saw several burnt-out hulls of large aircraft, probably abandoned airlines. Some military-type jet aircraft were also on the ground, the frames sticking out like rotting skeletons. They slowly drove down the runways and tarmacs, looking for the best choice. Finally, Sean pulled up to a fat, four-prop plane with Arabic words written on the sides. It was painted in a blue and white pattern. Sean pulled up close to the side, staying away from the wings, and left the van's engine running.

The plane reminded Brad of a C-130, but the nose didn't look right, and it was painted in civilian markings. The wheels and gear looked the same as a military heavy-lift plane, at least the kind Brad was accustomed to, but everything else was different. The plane sat alone on the edge of the tarmac with its cargo ramp down and support vehicles surrounding it. The crew door was swinging open above the wheeled portable walkway.

"What the hell kind of plane is this?" Nelson asked wearily.

Brooks jumped from the bed of the van before turning to help Brad out. "It's an Antonov AN-12, old Russian bird. They are pretty solid though, decent range. Nice choice if it'll fire up."

Kelli, their designated pilot, who had been riding in the cab and pointing out aircraft to Sean, quickly moved to the side of the aircraft and began an inspection. The rest of the men fanned out and began to set up a perimeter. "I think we are in luck, check this out," Kelli yelled from the back of the Antonov.

A large fuel truck was parked near the aircrafts' open rear ramp, and fuel hoses were still attached to the aircraft. A large yellow power unit was parked under the nose with cables running to the aircraft. Brad took his hand off of the side of the van and slowly limped toward the aircraft. He could see bodies scattered around the rear of the plane. "They must have been preparing to get out of Dodge when they were attacked," Kelli said.

Gunner looked at the bodies and scanned the horizon. "Certainly looks that way. Everyone stay sharp; I'm sure they are tucked into the shade, but they are here," Gunner warned. "Villegas, take a couple of men and clear the aircraft, try not to shoot it up too bad either, okay?"

The Villegas brothers nodded in response and ran up the portable walkway. Sean exited the van and went to the rear of the Antonov where Brad and Kelli had gathered. "Kelli, can you fly this?"

"I don't think it will be much of a problem. Obviously I don't have cert for it, but what the hell, right? I'm sure I can get it in the air, landing will suck though."

"How far can we go in this?"

"With the tanks topped off we can make Europe. I'm most familiar with the bases in Italy, so I'd like to plan for that."

"I'm giving you my team of wrenches, use them to get this thing off the ground, and train them to be your flight crew," Sean said.

"Roger that, Chief."

Brad went back to the van. He could see Kelli taking charge of Chelsea and the other Marines. She had them moving about smartly. Nelson headed to the power cart and began trying to get it operational. Villegas popped his head out of the crew entrance and announced that the plane was clear. Brooks ran to join Corporal Parker, who had slung his SAW over his back. Together they started transferring bags from the van to the cargo bay of the AN-12, being careful to make sure everything was properly secured.

Gunner and Sean were gathered near Brad looking over maps when Kelli reported to them. "Looks like the tanks are heavy with fuel. They were definitely prepping the aircraft for departure when it went down. Everything is set for takeoff. That is if your guy can get the power cart go–." The roar of a small engine cut her off midsentence as Nelson started the generator on the power cart.

"That settles that; I just need to make my way to the cockpit. We'll be ready to go in another twenty minutes," Kelli said.

"Okay, let's hustle. The CH-53 is due for pick up in less than an hour ... I'd like to be gone by then," Gunner said.

"What happens when we aren't there? Will they look for us? I don't want people to get hurt trying to find us," Brad asked.

"No, that won't happen. The CH-53 will loiter in the area as long as they have fuel. After that, they'll return to base. They have a no search and rescue order. They figure if a mob was big enough to take out a group, then it's too dangerous for a rescue," Gunner answered.

Brad squinted. "Damn, that's really messed up."

"Yes it is, but it works to our advantage today. How's that leg? Can you manage to get your ass on board? Or does somebody need to carry you?" Gunner said.

"I'll manage," Brad replied.

As Brad turned to hobble toward the aircraft's cargo ramp, they heard the sounds of suppressed gunfire. "Several contacts; north terminal!" Hahn yelled from the far side of the aircraft.

Sean stopped what he was doing and ran toward Hahn with his rifle in hand. Gunner grabbed the bags and started helping with the cargo transfer. "Lieutenant, we don't have twenty minutes, we need to go now!"

Brad stopped and grabbed the last bag from the back of the van. He sucked up the pain and half-jogged to the rear ramp. He tossed the bag into the aircraft and dropped into a prone position across the back of the ramp with his rifle. He could sense the commotion behind him as the others prepared the aircraft for takeoff. Brad pulled the remainder of the painkilling lollipop from his pocket and put it in his mouth. He adjusted his weight to his left side and relaxed into the optics of his rifle as the first wave of primals rounded a corner and came into view.

There were only ten of them, but they were running fast on a collision course for Sergeant Hahn and Specialist Theo, who had set up an observation post about one hundred meters out. The two men were between Brad and the mob and directly in Brad's line of fire. The soldiers were firing into the charging creatures. One at a time, a soldier would rapid fire while the other would leapfrog back. They were making good movements but the mob wasn't slowing down.

From his peripheral vision, Brad saw Sean take a position under a wing of the aircraft. Sean dropped to the ground and aimed his rifle downrange. He took quick shots, cutting down the lead runners. Sean's rifle fire allowed the soldiers to quicken their pace. They fell in alongside Sean just as the first of the four engines roared to life.

Now with the soldiers clear, Brad was able to take aimed shots at the advancing primals. He was surprised to be so focused even under the influence of the lollipop. He was even having a good time, he thought to himself, smiling. He fired rhythmically, knocking the charging crazies down. Not every round was a kill shot, but he did enough to put the primals on the ground and slow the attack.

A gunshot behind him broke Brad's focus. He turned to see Brooks firing directly to the rear of the aircraft at another mob that was closing in on them from the terminal. More gunfire started outside near where the van was parked, and Brad feared they were becoming surrounded. Brad adjusted his position to take line with Brooks as he saw Nelson and Craig run up the ramp, shouting that the start cart and ladder were clear.

Brad aimed and fired into the body of the mass of primals. He hit several of them square, but more filled the gaps. Corporal Parker and Gunner had joined them on the ramp and fired rapidly into the closing mob. Parker's loud unsuppressed M249 machine gun was sweeping and cutting down the advancing mob. Brad heard Sean shouting, "Three friendlies coming around!" as Sean, Hahn, and Theo climbed the high side of the ramp and rolled into the aircraft.

The throttles increased with the roar of the engines and the plane began to move forward. Chelsea worked a lever and the ramp began to rise, with the firing men still perched on the end of it. Brad stayed in position next to Brooks, firing until someone grabbed him by the good leg and dragged him into the cargo bay. A wave of primals collided with the ramp just as it closed. They could hear them banging against the aircraft's body as Kelli slowly taxied the AN-12.

Brad had been dragged onboard and near the pallet of rucksacks and gear. He grabbed at one and used it to unsteadily get to his feet. He moved forward and found Sean near a portside window. Brad strained for position and looked outside the aircraft. He could see an increasing stream of them pouring from hanger bays and buildings along the runway. Several had already gotten near the props and been chopped to pieces.

"Good thing this is a propeller job! Jet aircraft might have trouble swallowing all of those body parts," Sean said casually over the roar of the engines.

"Won't that mess up the blades?" Brad asked.

"I'm sure it's not good for them, but beats the hell out of the alternative," Sean said.

"Alternative?"

"Going back outside to fight them."

Kelli brought the AN-12 onto a cleared section of the runway and rolled to the end. She made a quick maneuver, spinning the plane around so that it faced down the long empty strip. The primals were still rushing from all directions but had stopped launching themselves at the aircraft and its props. They seemed to be confused, unsure of what to do with it, or how to get at the men inside. They had massed in a crowd around the plane but were giving it space to move.

The AN-12's engines roared up as they climbed to maximum power. Kelli released the brakes and the plane began to vibrate and speed forward down the runway. Brad suddenly lost his balance and reached out for leverage. "You should probably get strapped in, hero," Sean said, looking at Brad.

Brad turned to take a step toward the rows of seats filling the middle of the aircraft and almost fell. Sean caught him and dropped him into a seat. Brooks moved up beside them and took a seat as the plane rapidly rose into the air. They heard the gear come up and lock into place. Brad put his seat back and smiled.

"Anyone know what the in-flight meal will be?" Brad asked.

"Not sure about beef or chicken, but I still have that morphine for you," Brooks said.

31.

Burdened by heavy fur clothing, the bearded man wearily walked the trail. He distributed his weight on a walking stick to take pressure off of a nagging back. Jeremiah had followed the boys for more than five miles. His sons had something to show him, something they had found during their morning rounds. They had rushed back to the farm with excitement in their voices, dragging him out and onto the trail.

Jeremiah was still curious as to why his two teen sons had wandered so far from the pasture. They told him they were searching for a lamb; he had his doubts, but was too tired to argue with them. The previous night's winter storm had been harsh and scattered the flock, so the story was plausible. He knew they were young men and needed adventure in their lives. Jeremiah tried not to harass them; he knew that was their mother's job.

It was dangerous out in the hills away from the farm, especially with the cold of winter drawing in out of the high ground. He told his sons to stay close to the pastures. Still, it had been months since the last of the infected attacks, and the boys had become more complacent as a result of their boredom. He was sure they had wandered the path to visit their old school, now closed and shuttered. They were always in search of a school friend, or news from the outside.

He saw the boys standing and waiting for him at the top of a hill. They had said they found something; something he needed to see. They refused to tell him what, probably knowing he would refuse to go if he suspected danger. That was why he had followed them all the way out here on this cold fall day, humoring the boys and joining them on their adventure.

As Jeremiah neared the top of the hill, he could smell the smoke of a wood fire, and his senses went on high alert. Wood smoke could mean a campfire, and camp fires meant people. Not everyone was friendly these days. He checked his coat to make sure his old service pistol was still in his hip pocket as he hastened his pace up the hill. Jeremiah rounded the top, falling alongside his boys, and looked down into the snow-covered valley. He stood in awe at the sight.

A long, earth-strewn trench was sheared across the pasture. The trench ended at the smoking body of a large, destroyed aircraft. The nose of the plane was badly damaged; a wing and parts of engines lay behind the plane, impaled in the ground. The main body of the plane seemed intact from the distance atop the hill, but it had rolled to one side at an odd angle.

"See Dad, we told you! What is it?" Jeremiah's youngest son, Michael, asked.

The man stood staring at the wreckage. Fear struck him; maybe he should return to the farm, pretend he had never seen it.

No. There could be supplies on board, or possibly survivors.

Or infected.

"Anyone else hear tell of this??"

"Not a soul, Dad. We came right to ya," William answered.

"Stay close behind me boys, and keep those guns ready. Let's go have us a look," he said to them, already second-guessing his words. He turned and watched his boys ready the small double barreled, twenty-gauge shotgun and semi-automatic .22 rifle he had given them months earlier. He told them to keep their fingers off the triggers as he led them down toward the crash site.

Jeremiah thought his days of violence had ended when he left the service. Ten years in the Army, most of it with the 22nd regiment, had been enough for him. He happily left the forces and took over his father's farm. The Army service pistol had been a retirement gift from his old man. His father had also been a 22nd man. The pistol was the same one his grandfather had given to his father when he returned from Korea.

His boys were not new to the dangers of the world. They had survived their fair share of attacks by the infected. For the most part, their remote farm sheltered them from the dangers they had witnessed on the television. Thomas, his older boy, had been in the city during the first of the attacks and had barely made it home. He told of the behavior of the infected and warned how they attacked without mercy.

Days after the first outbreaks, a neighbor had come to him seeking help for his wife. She had been bitten. He tried for town, but the streets were blocked and the infected roamed freely. Jeremiah gave his neighbor all of the medical supplies he had. A day later his neighbor's family attacked them. They had killed one of his sheep, and had trapped his wife and son in the barn.

Jeremiah tried to reason with his longtime friend but he received a moan in response. They took their attention from the barn and charged at him. When the neighbor went to attack Jeremiah, he shot his neighbor three times in the chest with his old Army revolver. The man fell, but his neighbor's wife and daughter carried on with the attack. If Thomas hadn't been carrying the .22 rifle, they would have killed him.

Jeremiah approached from the nose of the aircraft. He could clearly see now that the cockpit had been destroyed. The plane listed heavily to the side with the missing wing. The other side of the plane had half a wing pointed up at the sky. They moved close to the plane and walked near the sheared-off half-wing. Fluids still dripped from the wreckage, and not much snow had accumulated on the hull. The wreckage had not been here long.

Jeremiah positioned his sons on a high embankment and warned them to cover him as he moved down to the rear of the aircraft. He could already see from his current position that the back half of the plane was split open. He was hoping he might be able to see or even enter the fuselage. Jeremiah watched his footing and walked steadily to avoid the crunching of the fresh snow. He had grown up hunting small game, and was familiar with stalking prey.

He removed the Army pistol from his pocket and felt the weight of it in his gloved hand. Jeremiah slowly moved toward the split in the aircraft's hull. The break was large, plenty large enough for him to step through if he could get high enough to access it. Jeremiah searched for a foothold but found none. He decided to try and climb to the break, but paused when he heard the sparrow's call: a warning from his sons.

Jeremiah turned back to make eye contact with the boys as a man stepped up beside him. Jeremiah was startled, and instinctively went to raise the pistol. Before he could, a second man moved in from behind him and quickly released it from his grip. Jeremiah took a clumsy step backwards, almost falling, before he was grabbed by the man and righted back to his feet.

He looked up into the bearded, toothy smile of a man in uniform. The man was dressed in tan camouflage and had a small sub machine gun strapped to his chest. Now well balanced, Jeremiah took a step back and turned on the large man standing behind him. He was dressed in the same camouflage pattern and carrying the same type of machine gun. Jeremiah looked up as another uniformed man, dressed in different camouflage, limped from around the tail of the aircraft followed by several others.

Jeremiah took another step back and put his hands in the air.

"Lard tunderin Jesus, b'y! Welcome to Newfoundland!"

Thank You for Reading
If you have an opportunity Please Leave a review on Amazon

Lundy W. J. (2013-10-31). Only the Dead Live Forever. Kindle Edition.
Whiskey Tango Foxtrot: Volume III
Visit W.J. Lundy on Facebook
Volume I Whiskey Tango Foxtrot. Kindle Edition.
Volume II Tales of the Forgotten. Kindle Edition.

Book four in the Series
In progress